August Nights

August Nights

A Sydney Bryant Mystery

Patricia Wallace

Five Star • Waterville, Maine

A Sydney Bryant Mystery

Five Star First Edition Mystery Series.

Published in 2002 in conjunction with Tekno-Books and Ed Gorman.

Set in 11 pt. Plantin by Christina S. Huff.

Printed in the United States on permanent paper.

Library of Congress Cataloging-in-Publication Data

Wallace, Patricia (Patricia Wallace Estrada).
    August nights : a Sydney Bryant mystery / Patricia Wallace.
        p. cm.—(Five Star first edition mystery series)
    ISBN 0-7862-4180-2 (hc : alk. paper)
    1. Women private investigators—California—San Diego—
    Fiction. 2. San Diego (Calif.)—Fiction. I. Title. II. Series.
PS3573.A42698 A93 2002
    813′.54—dc21   2002023273

For one heat, all know, doth drive out another,
One passion doth expel another still.

—George Chapman

Prologue

Tuesday

It was a sorry sight indeed, Xavier Walker thought. Surveying the abundance of greenery in the Waylaid Bar, he concluded that life in Southern California had transcended simple weirdness. Ferns all over the place, nature run amok under far too much artificial light. Used to be a bar looked like what it was meant to be—a place to get away from the confines of polite society—instead of a blooming botanical exhibit at the San Diego Zoo.

Worse yet, the place was jammed, crawling with up-and-comers, intense young men and a few grim-eyed women who were dressed for success. Or else.

Xavier sighed. Next time, he'd pick the place. Then again, maybe after turning fifty he'd mutated into one of those old fossils who were forever bemoaning the way things used to be. Time had a nasty way of passing, whether you liked it or not, and whatever couldn't keep pace was pretty much obsolete.

Including people.

A young pup with a razor cut and an attitude jostled him, getting by. "Hey, sorry," the pup said in a tone that clearly indicated otherwise.

"No problem," Xavier said with equal insincerity. He wasn't looking for trouble—standing a shade under five foot six, he seldom did—but neither was he about to take grief from one of this crowd. A punk like that wouldn't last a minute in a real bar.

Turning, he spotted a couple vacating a booth across the way and elbowed a path towards it. He slid into the cushioned seat a fraction of a second before a thirty-something bottle blonde reached the booth. "Age before beauty," he said.

The look she gave him nearly wilted the ivy on the wallpaper. "Then you certainly qualify," she said, turning on her heel.

Further evidence of the loss of civility. He pushed the ninety-five cents in change the prior occupants—and big spenders—had left as a tip to the edge of the table in the vain hope it would attract the waitress. She, presumably, would bus the table before he dragged a shirt sleeve through the myriad of water rings that bespoke a dazzling indifference to the State of California's former and future drought. After a moment, he added a crumpled dollar from his own pocket as enticement.

The Metro section of the local paper had been left on the table amid the clutter, and a headline above the fold caught his eye—SKELETAL REMAINS IDENTIFIED—with a dateline of Reno, Nevada.

A wave of nostalgia rolled over him.

In an earlier life, he'd spent seven years as a Washoe County deputy sheriff, based in Reno. He'd been married to his second wife, Belinda, in those days, and had a full head of hair. The hair was hardly more than a fond and distant memory now, which couldn't be said of Belinda and that ill-fated union. Although, like the cowboy he'd once fancied himself to be, after being thrown, stomped flat, and thoroughly trampled, he'd gotten right back in the saddle, and had married and divorced three, count 'em, *three* wives in the fifteen years hence. All else aside, he harbored a secret soft spot for Reno, the self-proclaimed Biggest Little City in the West.

As for the skeletal remains, the high desert was briskly efficient at reducing the human body to its bony infrastructure within weeks or even days. He'd read about a case some years back in which the police had erroneously concluded that a clutch of sun-bleached bones they'd found were too weathered to be those of a child who'd been missing for only a month or two. More than a year passed before anyone bothered to cross-check the cases and discover the tragic oversight.

Curiosity piqued, he scanned the three lines of text above the fold:

> A forensic anthropologist has identified a skull found in
> a remote area of Washoe County as that of a Reno man
> who has been missing since 1985.

Ah, 1985! He remembered it well, the year that marked the beginning of the end of his second attempt at wedded bliss. Belinda had turned into a casino bunny, hopping from one mirrored lounge to another, and her infidelities had triggered a marital meltdown, along with assorted financial disasters.

But he didn't blame that on Reno.

He was reaching for the paper to read further when Kathryn Bryant arrived. She was an attractive woman, with short gray hair and warm blue eyes, perhaps in her early sixties, but aging with an easy elegance that trivialized the eternal quest for—and worship of—youth.

"I hope you haven't been waiting long," she said.

"Not long. It took some fancy footwork to get out of the

9

office in mid-afternoon, particularly since I've got the Richardson surveillance tonight—"

"You don't think Sydney suspects, do you?"

Sydney was his partner in the newly incorporated Bryant & Walker Investigations, as well as a crackerjack investigator, and the reason for this hush-hush meeting. "It's hard to tell with your daughter, Kathryn. Not a lot gets by her. And she has a way of keeping what she knows to herself."

There was no mistaking the loving exasperation in Kathryn's eyes. "Doesn't she, though?"

"Still, I think I'm covered. So . . . what is it you want me to do?"

"I want to give Sydney a surprise bridal shower before the summer's over—"

Xavier shifted in his seat. "I don't mean to interrupt, but I wasn't aware that she and Mitch had actually set a date."

"No, you're right, they haven't," Kathryn said with a shake of her head, "for various unspecified reasons. Nevertheless, I am not content to sit idly by and wait forever for Sydney to get around to getting married. The girl needs a nudge."

Xavier said nothing. He was well aware of Kathryn's contention that Lieutenant Mitchell Travis was not, in fact, the right man for Sydney—and Ethan Ross was—so he found it a bit peculiar that she would do anything to promote a wedding . . . if that was what she really had in mind.

Sydney could be quietly devious if the situation warranted it. For all he knew, she'd inherited that particular trait from her mother.

"What I thought, Xavier, was that we should have it at the office on a Saturday afternoon—"

"Our office?" he asked uneasily.

"It's the perfect spot. We both know my workaholic daughter wouldn't hesitate to run to the office on some pretext or another. You'll think of something that requires her immediate attention, I'm sure."

"I will?"

Kathryn nodded. "Only when she opens the door, we'll yell 'Surprise!' "

He considered mentioning that Sydney had taken to wearing her .38 in a holster at the small of her back after an incident this past April, but decided it probably wasn't something a mother would want to hear. And he was reasonably certain that his partner was disciplined enough not to shoot on impulse.

"I'll need a key to the office, so we can decorate that morning. Nothing cute, mind you; Sydney has a low tolerance for cute. But I know of a florist who does the most breath-taking arrangements, works of art, really. We'll serve cake and champagne . . . that should put her in the mood, don't you think?"

In *a* mood, anyway.

As if belatedly aware of his silence, Kathryn hesitated, looking at him intently. "What do you think?"

"Well, it's . . . an idea, certainly." A crazy idea, he thought, with roughly one chance in a million of achieving the desired result.

Judging by her expression, she'd read his mind. "It won't work, will it?"

Xavier offered a rueful smile. "I'd be surprised if it did."

"I was afraid of that." She sighed. "I honestly don't know what to do."

Warning bells were ringing in his brain—it really was none of his business—but he couldn't resist asking, "Why do you have to do anything?"

11

"This . . . situation . . . with Sydney and Mitch and Ethan can't go on—"

The waitress arrived then and began to clear the table in the uncomfortable silence that followed. As she reached for the newspaper, Xavier grabbed it, folding it and tucking it into his inside jacket pocket. "Haven't read the funnies yet."

The waitress shrugged. "Are you ready to order?"

"A glass of Chardonnay, please," Kathryn said, a touch of melancholy in her voice.

He steeled himself against it; he did not care to involve himself in his partner's personal, private life. He had never been particularly adept at dealing with his own family dynamics, much less anyone else's. And he wasn't fool enough to rush in . . . not if he could help it. The question was, could he help it? Feeling a potential need to brace himself, he ordered a whisky sour, then thought better of it. "Make that," he amended, "a double."

By midnight, the whisky had worn off. The sour endured, churning in his stomach like battery acid. After his meeting with Kathryn, he had somehow fulfilled his duty to Sydney—not to mention their client—by keeping a close, if uneventful, watch on the Richardson residence. But as he trudged up the stairs to his second floor apartment, he felt the accumulated stress of the day weighing him down.

"Getting too old for this shit," he muttered, locking the door behind him a minute later. He tossed his keys on the table beside the entry, shrugged out of his jacket and tossed it over the back of the couch.

The folded newspaper he'd stuck in his pocket—and had promptly forgotten about—fell to the floor. Stiff after six hours of surveillance in a parked car, his back muscles protested as he went down to retrieve the paper, and he could hear his spine creak in delicate accompaniment to his popping knees.

Wonderful. Making his own sound effects.

He took the paper into the kitchen to make a cup of Sleepytime tea. As he waited for the water to boil, he ate a few low-sodium crackers to settle his stomach, and spread the paper on the kitchen table.

For a moment he blanked on what he was looking for, but then his eyes were drawn to the magic words: SKELETAL REMAINS IDENTIFIED.

"Ah yes, the bones." He squinted at the small print beneath the headline, looking for the name given to said bones. When he came to it, his flesh prickled with goose bumps.

It was a familiar name, albeit one he really hadn't expected to come across ever again. Although truth to tell, he had never bought the Sheriff's pet theory, back in the summer of 1985. And rightfully so, it turned out.

"Sean Foster," he said softly as the kettle began to whistle behind him. "I knew you didn't kill her."

One

With a hand on the deadbolt, Sydney Bryant took a peek through the peephole and was treated to a fish-eyed view of the back of her partner's head as he gazed down the empty, dimly lit hallway. Looking at what, she wondered, opening the door. "It's one o'clock in the morning."

"Another of your sterling qualities," Xavier said as he brushed by her, "you always know the time."

"I only mention it because it's a little late—"

"Indeed it is but, bless your heart, you're a night owl like myself, for which I am grateful, since I'm too wired to sleep."

"Wired, huh?" Sydney watched as he locked the front door, and noticed his hands were shaking slightly. "Is there anything wrong?"

"Not that I need as much sleep as I used to," he said, ignoring the question. "And why should I? I got plenty of beauty sleep in my youth and I look like this anyway, so I ask myself, why bother?"

"Xavier—"

He turned, frowning. "I'm sorry, what?"

"Do you want to tell me what has you so wired in the middle of the night?"

His expression was blank, as though he wasn't really seeing her, as though he were a million miles away . . . and then he kind of shook himself and his demeanor changed abruptly, from near-manic to cool and dispassionate. "I need to talk to you. It's urgent, or I wouldn't bother you."

"So talk."

"Can I sit down?"

"Be my guest," she said, and followed him into the living room, where he sat for all of three seconds before he got up and began to pace. Noting the sheen of perspiration on his forehead, she frowned. He looked pale, not a good sign in a man of his age. "Is something wrong? Don't tell me Richardson showed up at the house—"

"Who?"

"You know, the guy we were hired to watch out for?" At his blank look, she added, "The one who's trying to make off with his kids."

"Oh, him. No, no, nothing like that."

"Thank God," Sydney said under her breath, and sank onto the couch.

Xavier continued to pace, evidently oblivious, and then stopped suddenly, squinting fiercely, as though deep in thought, flexing his fingers like a pianist limbering up to play, lips moving without sound. Talking to himself.

It was, Sydney suspected, a professional hazard; she did it all the time, for the simple reason that what you never uttered out loud could never come back to haunt you—

Xavier turned on his heel and pointed a finger at her. "You have to go."

Startled, she laughed. "Hey, I live here."

"To Reno."

"Excuse me?"

He ran a hand over his bald pate. "On the drive over, I was trying to figure out how I could get away to do this myself, but I'm under subpoena in the Dreyer case."

15

The Dreyer case was a spectacularly nasty divorce action that had escalated to include charges of aggravated assault and battery, as well as trespass, vandalism, resisting arrest, and discharging a weapon within city limits. Xavier was a vital prosecution witness, since the weapon had been aimed in his general direction when fired.

"I *have* to testify or risk contempt of court and a bench warrant for failure to appear," he said. "But you can go in my place—"

"To Reno?"

"I'll give you my old case files to review. I kept everything, so getting up to speed shouldn't be a problem."

"Xavier—"

"I've got clippings from the local news coverage at the time, a bit yellowed but readable, and I think even videotape, if it hasn't deteriorated too badly over the years. Plus, of course, copies of the crime scene photographs."

"Hold on." Sydney signaled time out. "What files? What case? What crime scene?"

"Fifteen years ago, a beautiful young woman named Laura Foster was murdered on her wedding day." There was a curiously haunted expression in his eyes. "I was the first officer at the scene. I was the one who found her."

Clearly, he had been unable to forget it.

"They never caught the killer. If you want my opinion, they were looking for the wrong man from day one. Now there's been a major development in the case—"

"This is an *active* murder case?"

"It is now." Xavier took off his glasses and rubbed at his eyes. "But not for long, my dear, because you are going to take up where I left off."

"Where you left off as a law enforcement officer," she reminded him, "in performance of your sworn duty. Murder is a police matter. An out-of-state police matter."

"Well, yes, technically."

"I believe the operative word here is *legally*."

"Ah, Sydney, arguing semantics," he said and tsked. "And with a straight face."

"I won't deny I've worked murder cases, but I'm sure the last thing anyone in Reno wants is a private investigator from California nosing around."

"They'll get over it. In point of fact—" Xavier winked at her—"we've already been hired."

"What?"

"Make me a cup of tea, why don't you, and I'll fill you in on the details."

Sydney scrounged though her kitchen cupboards and found a box of China Oolong tea bags. After brewing a cup for Xavier, she grabbed a Pepsi for herself and sat down across from him. "Tell me," she said.

"Don't worry, I will. The thing is, someone could read through the paperwork and never get a real sense of what it was like that day. I want to tell you how it went down . . . and the way she looked."

Sensing that he was waiting for a go-ahead, she nodded.

"It was near twilight on a Saturday, the first week of August, 1985. Hot as hell, naturally, but a dry heat. There were storm clouds to the west, over the Sierra, and the wind was blowing like the devil.

"I was three hours into my shift, cruising the back roads. As hot as it gets in the summer, it's not unusual to come across a stranded motorist now and again, vapor-locked on the shoulder. Once in awhile some poor moron will ignore his temperature gauge and actually go up in flames, but that shift, as I recall, started out nice and quiet."

Watching him, she saw a subtle change in his face, a hardening, as though he were steeling himself for what was to come.

"It didn't stay quiet . . ." His voice trailed off. "I remember thinking that there was something *stirring* in the air."

Sydney knew that feeling all too well.

"Strange as it may seem, I was up for it. Shit, back then, I was an adrenaline junkie. Flashing lights and sirens screaming in the night . . . there's no better rush than that."

Once upon a time, she might have agreed.

"I came around a bend in the road," he said, "and saw a Mustang parked with the hood up, radiator steaming, and both doors standing wide open. 'Just Married' was painted on the rear window in big white letters. Don't ask me why or how, but when I saw that, I knew there was trouble."

An indefinable quality in his voice sent a shiver down her spine.

"I pulled over and parked maybe twenty feet behind the Mustang, in case there were tire tracks or footprints or other evidence in the vicinity of the vehicle. Preserving the scene." He smiled bleakly. "Listen to me, would you? I still sound like a cop."

"Once a cop—"

"—always a cop, I know. Anyway, I radioed in to Dispatch, gave 'em the plate to run. While they were doing that, I got out and walked over to a spot in the road where I could look into the car."

Sydney could easily imagine it: a trim young Xavier in uniform, walking slowly along a deserted road, one hand reaching to unfasten his holster, fingers absently stroking the smooth wooden grip of his gun . . .

"On the front passenger seat was a bridal bouquet. Pink roses, the tiny ones, with white lace and a pink ribbon. I remember looking at the roses and getting a cold feeling in the pit of my stomach."

"You didn't see anyone?"

"Not a soul. Didn't hear anything either, other than the hiss of steam. Out in the desert, there's usually a kind of insectile *hum* in the background, grasshoppers or what-not, that you hear on a subliminal level but that you're not really aware of until it stops."

"That's kind of . . . spooky."

"It was that, and more." Xavier took a sip of tea and made a face, as though it—or the memory—were bitter. "I was hyper-alert, let me tell you. The juices were flowing. I called out, but no one answered. I walked around to the front of the car and called again. Then I saw her.

"She was maybe fifty yards up the road, and another fifty to the south of it, partially hidden behind the sagebrush. The only reason I spotted her that quickly was because of the wind; it caught at her dress and the skirt was fluttering . . ."

Fate, Sydney thought, in yet another guise.

"Then I saw the blood," Xavier said. "A *lot* of blood. Seeing that, I figured she had to be mortally wounded, either dying or dead."

Sydney realized that she was holding her breath, and let it out in a sigh.

"A second later, I swear to God, I thought I saw her move. My first impulse was to go to her, but I . . . because the place was so isolated, because it would take so long to get help out there, I ran back to the patrol unit first. I radioed for medical assistance and grabbed the first aid kit out of the trunk."

It was almost certainly the correct procedure under the circumstances, but Xavier's expression indicated he felt otherwise.

"First aid my ass." He shook his head, disgusted. "As if a

roll of gauze and a bottle of Mercurochrome would make a whit of difference—"

Sydney reached across the table and covered his hand with hers. "A surgeon might not have made a difference."

"You're probably right, but that hasn't made it any easier to live with. She was dead when I got to her, but I've always wondered, if I'd gotten there even a few seconds earlier . . ."

Sydney squeezed his hand.

"The human thing to do would've been to go to her, period. What if she was hanging on somehow, waiting for help? I'm not delusional, I know I couldn't have saved her, but at least she wouldn't have died alone."

"Xavier, don't."

"At least I could have held her hand." Turning his hand over, he closed his fingers around hers. "This much, I could have given her. A little comfort as she was dying. A human touch."

Which explained why this case was so important to him. "You did what you could."

"It wasn't enough. They say regrets never change anything, but mine changed me." Husky-voiced, he cleared his throat. "She was dead when I reached her; there wasn't a pulse. Her lips were parted but she wasn't breathing. Her face was unmarked. Looking at her—she was so beautiful—I could almost believe that she was just sleeping."

The ultimate, final sleep, Sydney thought. "How was she killed?"

"She'd been stabbed, repeatedly. There were the defense wounds on her arms and to her hands—the web of her right thumb and index finger had been sliced all the way to the bone—but the significant damage was to her chest. The final coroner's report indicated eight or nine penetrating wounds in or near the heart, any one of which could have proved fatal."

Although she was no stranger to the graphic findings in postmortem reports, she winced. "Sounds like overkill."

"That doesn't *begin* to cover it. Laura Foster was slaughtered," he said vehemently, a dark glimmer in his eyes. "She bled to death, discarded off the side of the road like so much trash."

For a moment, neither of them spoke.

At that precise instant, Sydney decided to take the case.

Two

When she arrived at the office at a quarter to eight on Wednesday morning, Sydney found a battered, slightly dusty box of files on her desk, a note from Xavier taped diagonally across the top. Printed in bold block letters, the note read:

Syd:

> *The answer is in here somewhere. If anyone can uncover the truth, it's you. And I was wrong about needing my beauty sleep. Caught a glimpse of the old kisser in the mirror, scared the stuffing out of myself.*
>
> *I'll be in later today. In the meantime, dig in.*
>
> *Bon appetit,*
> *The X-Man*

Sydney sighed, peeling the paper from the box and crumpling it into a wad. She banked it cleanly off the wall into the far wastebasket, a three-point shot.

"That's talent, baby," she cheered, doing a rather lame impression of sportscaster Dick Vitale as she opened the cardboard flaps. Crammed inside were a dozen or so bulging folders, a well-used inter-office envelope with a string and button closure, and an expanding file secured with a frayed elastic band.

On top was a gray plastic case that, she verified, contained a videotape. A red-bordered label on the case identified the tape as consisting of "News footage, Laura Foster, Homicide."

A little early in the day for that, she thought, selecting instead a folder marked Police Reports and sitting down to read.

Ten pages into the file, Sydney had read enough to strongly suspect that Xavier might be right: from the very outset, the police had zeroed in on Sean Foster as their one and only suspect. They had quickly concluded that because the victim's husband was missing from the murder scene, he was implicated in her death. They hadn't considered the possibility that he might also be a victim of foul play.

Proof of that was evident in the fact that the search for Sean Foster had focused on so-called 'getaway' routes. The police had immediately issued an All Points Bulletin, notifying other law enforcement agencies and security at the international borders, as well as airports, bus depots, and train stations, to be on the lookout for anyone matching his description. The Bulletin itself suggested the missing bridegroom was "probably armed" and warned the public "Do not approach the suspect."

All the while, the poor guy was dead. And dead guys, as a rule, are relatively easy to catch.

An argument could be made that the police investigators were functionally hindered by what psychologists referred to as "confirmation bias," since they had actively pursued only those leads which were likely to confirm their theory of the murder. By definition, that implied they had—willfully or not—disregarded whatever evidence did not conform with the scenario which evolved from that theory.

Under those circumstances, impartiality hadn't a chance.

Sydney had reserved a ticket on an afternoon flight to Reno and was working her way through the alphabet soup of hotels when Hannah DeWilde, Bryant & Walker Investigations' recently acquired secretary *extraordinaire,* showed up at eight-thirty.

"You're in bright and early this morning," Hannah noted a few minutes later as she brought in a sheath of transcribed status reports.

"Early, yes. Bright might be pushing it."

Hannah offered a sympathetic smile. "The weekend will be here soon."

"With any luck, I'll be off the phone by then." She tucked the receiver between her shoulder and ear, accepted the reports along with a pen, and began signing on the dotted line. "I seem to be stuck on perpetual hold in search of a room. There's some kind of a Fifties event going on in Reno, and the hotels are booked solid."

"Fifties? Do you mean seniors?"

"I think decade. The 1950s. Classic cars, sock hops, and poodle skirts, or so they tell me."

Hannah made a face. "And I quote: 'Those who cannot remember the past are condemned to repeat it.' "

"Possibly, but at least *they* have a room."

"Why don't I do that for you?" Hannah offered. "I used to work for a travel agent who could produce a vacancy out of thin air."

"In that case—" Sydney grinned, handing her the phone "—knock yourself out."

The San Diego Police Department was headquartered

downtown in a seven-story building on 14th and Broadway. Attractive for a government facility, its green and off-white exterior was complemented by smoked glass windows, which imparted a sense of discreet urgency and solemnity to the business conducted within.

The first floor housed the roll call and computer rooms, in addition to the booking area. It was often hectic, and on a summer day, Sydney expected to find the place swarming with police officers, irate citizens, and the occasional suspect, but when she arrived shortly after nine, the only person in sight was the desk officer. The brass nameplate over his left shirt pocket identified him as O'Leary.

A virtual poster-boy for ruddy-faced Irish cops, O'Leary did not look up from his crossword puzzle until she announced herself at the desk.

"I'm here to see Lieutenant Travis."

"You have an appointment?" he inquired, putting aside a bite-marked pencil and reaching for the phone.

In response, she nodded and handed him her business card. She hadn't bothered making an appointment, but figured it unlikely that Mitch would rat her out.

And he didn't: a moment later, O'Leary directed her to the elevator.

When the elevator opened to reveal not only Mitch, but Ethan Ross awaiting her, her instinct was to hit the button and close the doors again. Rationality prevailed, however, and she stepped out to join them in the hallway, an unwilling side to the triangle. "Ethan, this is a surprise."

Dressed for court in a navy blue pinstripe suit, white shirt, burgundy silk tie and tasseled loafers, Ethan arched an eyebrow in that mildly infuriating way he had, and smiled. "I imagine it must be."

A typical understatement, given that Ethan and Mitch, although once partners on the force, had fallen out—over her, to her deep and lasting regret—and now rarely spoke. Then again, Ethan was the quintessential lawyer, and had an attorney's gift for artful inference, leaving all manner of things unsaid.

Sydney glanced at Mitch, to no avail: he likewise had perfected the requisite a-professional-cop-never-reveals-what-he's-thinking look. It was all so civilized. Anyone passing by just now would never guess that beneath this polite facade, emotions were near the flash point.

Knowing better, she asked, "Am I interrupting?"

"Not at all; I was just on my way out." Ethan hesitated before offering his hand to Mitch. "I appreciate your time this morning; my office will be in touch."

"Glad I could help," Mitch said.

A soft *ding* and the elevator doors slid open again. She felt a momentary relief that the encounter was over. Except, of course, it wasn't.

As he passed by, Ethan gave her a searing look that was probably illegal in half a dozen Southern states. And if it wasn't, it ought to be.

"I'll call you, Sydney. We need to talk."

The problem with living in an area rife with earthquake faults was that, however sincerely you might wish for it, a bottomless crevasse seldom opened up to swallow you at a time when disappearing off the face of the earth would be most appreciated.

Like now.

Beside her, Mitch remained silent, asserting his territorial claim by stroking, ever so lightly, the inside of her wrist.

"Sure," she managed to say, "call me."

"Why, pray tell, would anyone take a case in Nevada?" Mitch asked, unlocking the door to an interrogation room and holding it open for her. "In the middle of the summer, no less."

"Let's just say it's an interesting case, and I'm intrigued."

Mitch caught her hand as she went by. Following her inside, he closed the door, leaned against it and pulled her to him.

Not that she resisted.

"Don't I intrigue you?"

"Lieutenant, please."

"Gets awfully hot in Reno this time of year." He kissed her on the neck and nuzzled his way to her ear. "Sizzling, in fact."

"It's pretty warm here, too." Acutely aware that the door didn't lock from the inside *and* of the observation room behind the two-way mirror that took up most of the far wall, Sydney gently pulled away, putting a little distance between them.

Mitch stayed where he was, a smile playing at the corners of his mouth as he adjusted his shoulder holster. The pearl gray shirt he wore accentuated his dark good looks, a striking contrast to his black hair and hazel eyes. "Come here," he said.

"In your dreams, Lieutenant."

His smile was tantalizing, seductive. "I do dream about it, every night."

"So do I."

Neither of them moved. The last thing she needed was for one of the other detectives to walk in and find them in a clinch. Engaged or not, she was aware that there was a fair amount of speculation about them circulating within the department. And while she had little faith in the oft-cited "reasonable expectation of privacy" the law theorized as being every citizen's right, neither was she naive enough to recklessly fan the flames.

"Weather aside," she said, determinedly changing the subject, "I've already taken the case. I'm flying out this afternoon."

"That soon?"

"No time to waste. As it is, I'll be fifteen years late arriving at the crime scene."

"This is a murder case, I take it?"

"Yes." It didn't surprise her that he would reach that conclusion, since murder was one of the few crimes not subject to the statute of limitations. She sat on a corner of the table, absently toying with the chain used to restrain handcuffed suspects as she outlined what she'd learned so far. "Suffice it to say, this one is quite a challenge."

"Sounds like it."

"I haven't read all of the reports yet, but Xavier told me a couple of things last night that really piqued my interest."

"Such as?"

"Laura Foster wasn't wearing a wedding ring when he found her. She'd gotten married that afternoon, only a few hours before she was killed. A blushing bride, minus a ring . . . that bothers me."

Mitch moved away from the door, finally, and came to sit beside her. "I don't know, kid. It's a little too Hollywood for my taste; in the real world, that sort of detail usually turns out to be meaningless."

"Maybe, but the missing ring was pivotal in convincing the homicide honchos—as Xavier so charmingly calls them— that her husband killed her."

He brushed her hair back from her face, his fingertips grazing her cheek. "Before the wedding night?"

Hearing the teasing tone in his voice, Sydney met his eyes. "Maybe he was worried that he couldn't fulfill her expectations."

"Ouch."

"Whatever the timing, the missing ring is symbolic." She paused, frowning. "The thing is, who else would have a reason to take it, if not Sean?"

"I gather Sean is the aforementioned missing and wrongly accused husband?"

"Is there any other kind? Except that he was missing *and* dead. And, ultimately, innocent."

"You think."

"I think and hope to prove," she said, and sighed. "Not that it will be easy. The attack was extremely vicious, which suggests it was personal."

"Hmm. You always hurt the one you love?"

"Something like that."

Mitch caught her off guard, kissing her suddenly. "I swear to God, Sydney, I will never let anyone hurt you."

Outside the interrogation room, phones were ringing and she could hear the soft murmur of conversation, but for the moment, she didn't care. She touched his face, gently tracing the scar on his chin with her fingertips, and then kissed him.

The man took her breath away.

Three

The rest of the morning passed in a rush of errands and phone calls, interrupted by a quick trip home to pack. As a result of Hannah's concerted efforts to clear her schedule for the week, Sydney made it to the airport in time to catch her plane.

Although an infrequent flyer, she had formed an opinion about the process, and did not rank Lindbergh Field on her top ten list of airports, due primarily to the fact that takeoffs were always to the west, in the direction of the Pacific. Air safety statistics aside, she found racing down the runway and heading straight for the ocean to be a vaguely disquieting experience.

Every time she'd flown out of San Diego, she got what could only be called a sinking sensation at the prospect of the plane losing thrust and falling belly first into the surf. She thought it highly unlikely that the engineers who designed aircraft had intended the machine to ride a wave or—in the beach scene vernacular—shoot the curl.

Not that slamming into terra firma was a more appealing prospect. It was, she mused, a good thing that passengers weren't equipped with black boxes to record *their* final moments of flight.

The skies might not be all *that* friendly, but gravity was a bitch.

Which was why, taking off, she closed her eyes and willed the plane aloft. As it banked to the right, gaining altitude still, she experienced a momentary weightlessness. Her stomach felt a little queasy, and she was grateful that she hadn't eaten lunch.

Five minutes later, when the attendant came around to take drink orders, she skipped her usual soft drink and asked for water instead.

Loathe as she was to waste in-flight time, she took the opportunity to review the dossier on Douglas Foster which she'd happened upon in Xavier's files. Foster was the uncle who'd raised Sean and his older brother, Alan, after their parents died in a single car rollover along an isolated stretch of Nevada highway in 1968. The same accident had gravely injured Foster, who reportedly had been sleeping in the back seat and was thrown from the car.

After two weeks in a coma, Douglas Foster awoke to find that he was a paraplegic, but was later quoted in a yellowed newspaper clipping as saying that he considered himself "the lucky one."

Being confined to a wheelchair hadn't kept him from making an incredible fortune in biotech: his privately held company, CardioPulse, manufactured pacemakers, artificial heart valves, and ventricular assist devices. On the cutting edge of technology and responsive to the demands of the market as only an independent company can be, CardioPulse had posted profits in excess of a billion dollars in the most recent fiscal year.

Never married, Foster had seemingly devoted himself to raising his brother's children. Included in the files were photographs of him with the boys at various ages on baseball diamonds, tennis courts, and other fields of play, the three of them smiling as though smiling were an Olympic event in which they hoped to medal.

A happy family?

Evidently so, since Douglas Foster was the one who had hired them to re-investigate the case. According to what Xavier had said last night, Foster had never doubted Sean's innocence for a moment, and was eager to clear his nephew's name.

To that end, she had an appointment to meet with him later this afternoon.

Looking out the window as the plane descended, Sydney was surprised at how green Reno appeared from the air. For a high desert town, there was a remarkable abundance of trees. Nestled in a meadow valley, with the Sierra-Nevada Mountains rising majestically off to the west—and brown, rolling hills everywhere else—Reno looked like an oasis in an otherwise arid landscape.

It didn't hurt that the sky was an impossible shade of blue. Crystal clear and of a darker hue than she remembered ever seeing in California, even as a child, it stirred her in a way she couldn't define.

As hectic as her morning had been, as little sleep as she'd gotten last night, she felt herself relax, anticipating touchdown.

". . . temperature is ninety-two degrees," the flight attendant was saying. "Enjoy your stay in Reno, and thank you for flying with us today."

The Reno-Tahoe airport was blessedly uncrowded, and Sydney easily found her way to the Hertz counter, where she rented a Ford Probe at the weekly rate, using the Agency's new corporate credit account—a welcome change from having to max out her personal Visa card. She walked the short distance to the baggage carousel a few minutes later, retrieved her suitcase, surveillance kit, video equipment, and the rest of Xavier's files—locked in an over-sized leather attaché—and enlisted the aid of a skycap, who loaded everything into the Probe's relatively spacious trunk.

Tipping the skycap ten dollars earned her a beaming, gap-toothed smile, as well as detailed directions to a real estate office on Virginia Street, where she had to go to sign the paperwork and charge slip for the time-share condominium that Hannah somehow had managed to arrange for her in lieu of a hotel room.

A quick excursion on and off the 395 freeway, and she was coasting down the long exit ramp to South Virginia in the right turn lane. Glancing in her rearview mirror as she stopped in the yield lane to wait for a break in the traffic, she was bemused to see a black Model T Ford directly behind her, while to her left, idled a peach-colored 1955 Chevy Bel Air, complete with fuzzy dice.

The Chevy's windows were down, and she could hear music which she recognized as Buddy Holly's impudent hit, "That'll Be The Day."

"It's a time warp," she said under her breath. Every hotel clerk she'd talked to this morning had informed her about Hot August Nights—the classic cars, in particular—but seeing was believing.

Behind her, the Model T honked, no doubt impatient to hurry back to the past.

And the past was everywhere, it seemed.

"Enjoy your stay in Reno," the middle-aged but pony-tailed receptionist at the realty office chirped, handing her two white-tagged keys, an automatic garage door opener, and a blown-up city map. Dressed in striped pedal pushers, a white blouse with a Peter Pan collar, rolled bobby sox and brown-and-white saddle shoes, the woman had embraced the Fifties look with a vengeance. Judging by her make-up, she had also cornered the market on powder blue eye shadow. "And have fun, you hear?"

"Thanks, I will," she said, turning to leave.

"Oh, and if you need a dress for the prom, honey," the receptionist said, squinting as though perplexed at her jeans, moccasins and silk tee, "there's a store in town that rents them."

Sydney smiled. "I'll keep that in mind."

Walking back to the car, she noticed the heat for the first time. She'd parked in the shade, but even so, the seat was scorching when she got in. The steering wheel was too hot to touch, much less steer with.

The obvious solution was to avoid touching anything until it cooled off. She started the engine and turned the air conditioner on full blast, then took a few minutes to study the map and get her bearings.

She had to meet Douglas Foster at the Steakhouse in Harrah's at five-thirty. The dashboard clock read 4:03 P.M.

She'd be cutting it close, but the condo was only a little out of her way. There wouldn't be time to do much more than drop off her luggage and equipment, and maybe splash cold water on her face, but she preferred that to leaving thousands of dollars' worth of the Agency's property unattended in the trunk of the car.

Living in San Diego had instilled in her a healthy concern—arguably bordering on paranoia—regarding car theft. Just last week, a friend of hers named Victor Griffith had the unsettling experience of watching his rusting and decrepit

Dodge van being driven away after he'd hopped out and left the motor running while he ran into a 7-Eleven for a Big Gulp.

The van's muffler had fallen off when the thief drove over the center divider as he pulled a U-turn in the road while making his getaway. All that was left was a choking cloud of black exhaust.

As a reporter, Victor had a way of whittling every event down to a headline. In this case, his take on it was, "People will steal anything."

Which was slightly more cynical than her own world view, but in a strange town, she thought it prudent not to risk it, if for no other reason than she didn't have time to replace lost equipment.

A prom dress she could get, but it was probably a safe bet that there wasn't a store in town where she could replace night-vision binoculars equipped with a microphone wand, fiber optic mini-surveillance cameras, or any of the other high-tech toys increasingly common to the detective business.

The decision made, she pulled out of the realty parking lot and headed north on South Virginia.

The condo was another pleasant surprise. It was tastefully furnished in a quasi-Japanese style, with polished wood floors, sleekly designed black furniture with jade green cushions, and elegant floral screens that provided for little islands of solitude in every room.

There were three stories, with the living room, dining area and kitchen on the second floor, above the garage. The two bedrooms were on the top floor, each with a full bath. The master bedroom had a private balcony as well, accessible via French doors.

"Hannah," she said, stopping for a moment to gaze at the view of the Reno skyline from the balcony, "you're getting a raise."

It took three trips to stash everything in the entry closet, and then she was out of time. She locked up and ran back down the front stairs to the car.

Anxious now to get on with it and get to work, she swung the Probe in a tight arc around the cul-de-sac, and headed downtown.

Four

"When they told me the remains had been identified, and it was Sean, I'm not ashamed to admit that I broke down and cried," Douglas Foster said, swirling the red wine in his glass. "It hurt to find out my nephew was dead, but on the other hand, it wasn't totally unexpected. I never believed he was on the run, which meant that more than likely, he was a victim, too. But now Sean can be laid to rest . . . along with all of the suspicion and rumors."

Sydney nodded her understanding but said nothing, intent on taking the measure of this man. There was a quality to his voice—an edge—that suggested he had come to terms with his pain, but would not easily forgive whomever was the cause of it.

He wasn't anyone she would care to have as an enemy, she thought, watching him. Foster had the pampered, well groomed, and impatient look that she associated with obscene wealth, from his manicured nails to his impeccably styled silver hair. His gray Armani suit was a shade lighter than his shirt, his tie a shade darker. Such monochromic harmony did not result from chance, she was certain, given that his eyes were also gray in color.

Beyond appearances, she detected in those eyes a determination and singularity of purpose that was unnerving. Whatever his physical limitations, Douglas Foster impressed her as being tenacious and focused.

"Of course," Foster said, lowering his voice as the waiter discreetly removed the dessert plates, "the police deny that Sean's death changes anything. Except that now the case is officially closed."

"They told you that?" It would make her job simpler if she didn't have to worry about interfering in an active homicide investigation.

"Absolutely. Their position is that Sean committed suicide after he murdered Laura, out of guilt or remorse for what he'd done, or possibly from fear that he'd be caught."

"Have they any proof of that?"

"Not that I'm aware of." Foster took a sip of wine. "It would seem the sheriff's department has an institutionalized aversion to admitting they made a mistake."

"Were they able to determine a cause of death?"

"A gunshot to the head, presumably. They contend that it was self-inflicted, but of course with only the skull, there's no way they can prove it."

"Which means it's unlikely we could *disprove* it," Sydney noted, curious as to how he would react. She'd had clients in the past who refused to tolerate any viewpoint but their own, however insupportable that might be.

Foster appeared unperturbed. "As you say. Except I knew Sean, and they did not. The boy was madly in love with Laura. He didn't kill her, and he sure as hell didn't kill himself."

"My understanding is that there was an altercation on the day they were married. The day Laura died."

"An altercation? I suppose you could call it that." He paused, smiled sadly and shook his head. "Are you married, Ms. Bryant?"

"No."

"Ever been?"

"No."

"An attractive young woman like yourself, surely you've been in love?"

She smiled, but didn't answer.

"None of my business, I know, but I'll take that as a yes. You must know how mercurial love is, how illogical it can be."

"I won't argue with that," she said. There was a wistful expression in Foster's eyes that made her wonder at his own romantic past.

"Laura was the most beautiful bride I think I've ever seen. She had an ethereal beauty, a delicacy. The camera loved her—she wanted to be an actress—but a camera could never do justice to that face."

He sounded almost smitten himself.

"Sean was only twenty-four, and a young twenty-four at that. Young men are prone to jealousy. After the wedding, I held a small, private reception for the newlyweds at my home." A crease formed between his eyebrows. "I'll concede Sean may have had too much to drink; my nephew was given to excess in many of his personal habits. Anyway, there was music playing, and Sean took offense at the . . . well . . . the suggestive way that Laura was dancing with Randy—"

"And Randy is?"

"Sean's cousin, on his mother's side."

"What's his last name?" Sydney asked, opening her notebook to a blank page.

"Leighton," he said, and spelled it. "I don't want you to get the wrong idea about this. Randy was only sixteen or seventeen at the time, but the kid could dance. He and Laura were showing off, slow dancing, very close . . . I won't pretend it wasn't provocative."

"Which annoyed Sean."

Foster nodded. "And yet, it didn't amount to much. Sean

gave Randy a shove . . . they exchanged a few words. Alan and Gary stepped in before it got out of hand."

"I know Alan is Sean's older brother," she said, looking up from her notes, "but who is Gary?"

"Gary West was the best man. He and Sean had been friends since grade school. Anyway, he took Sean outside to cool off and that was that."

"The police report also states that Sean and Laura were overheard quarreling. In his statement, one of your guests, Brad Goldwyn, said he witnessed what the report refers to as 'a heated discussion' between the bride and groom."

Foster laughed.

It wasn't the reaction she'd expected, but neither did it surprise her. If she'd learned anything since she'd become an investigator, it was that no one was entirely predictable.

"So it was Goldwyn doing the trash-talking to the police. I always wondered where that particular tidbit came from. The cops refused to tell me; I think they were afraid I would try to buy off their precious informant."

"It isn't true?"

"Damned if I know. It could be. As I said, Sean had been drinking, and Laura . . . Laura was something of a flirt. I personally have no knowledge of any bickering between them that afternoon, but I wasn't with the wedding party all of the time." The crease between his eyes deepened. "Ever since the accident, I tire easily and without warning. I needed to rest and went to my room."

He did not strike her as the type of man who would seek or welcome sympathy for his plight, so she kept her tone matter-of-fact. "How long were you away?"

"An hour, perhaps a little longer."

Long enough, she thought. "What was the relationship between Brad Goldwyn and Sean?"

"There was none. Brad was a guest of Laura's. One of her two guests, I should say."

"Only two?"

"She was estranged from her family. As I recall, they were quite religious, what you might call fundamentalists, and they didn't approve of her ambition to act."

"Was she a local girl?"

Foster shook his head. "I believe she was from Maine or Vermont, somewhere in the east. As I recall, an uncle flew into town to take her home for burial. I'm sorry, but I don't know much more than that."

"How did she wind up in Reno? Correct me if I'm wrong, but Nevada isn't usually regarded as a hot-bed of opportunity for an aspiring actress."

"Well . . . there are opportunities of a sort."

It didn't require advanced math skills to put two and two together. "She was a showgirl?"

"Yes, but only briefly."

"Is that how she and Sean met?"

"No, no. Alan introduced them." Foster hesitated, and smiled uneasily. "To be frank, Alan was seeing Laura at the time. They met at a party and dated for a couple of weeks before he brought her home."

"That sounds like it could have been trouble."

"Could have been, but wasn't. When he realized that Laura was interested in Sean and vice versa, Alan behaved like the gentleman I raised him to be: he stepped aside and bowed out gracefully."

"With no hard feelings?"

Foster's smile turned cryptic. "Alan did not discuss his feelings with me, Ms. Bryant, nor would I have expected him to."

That was the difference between them, Sydney thought;

she would *ask* . . . and then do her utmost to verify whatever he told her through an independent source. "All right. Tell me about the other guests."

"Ah, let's see. There were nine of us for brunch, I remember that much . . ."

Skimming her notes, she could account for seven of the nine. The other names might or might not be listed in the police reports—she hadn't yet finished her review of the files—but she wanted Foster's input on everyone who'd attended the reception. To jog his memory, she asked, "Who was Laura's second guest?"

"Well, a friend of hers obviously. A rather exotic creature with an improbable name which has unfortunately just now slipped my mind—"

"Male or female?"

"Female, a little wisp of a thing. She dressed like a gypsy, came to the wedding in a costume that looked as if she'd pinned it together out of scarves. She had dozens of cheap silver bracelets on each wrist, plus truly horrid rings—in the shape of snakes, spiders, and lizards—on every grubby finger. And she was barefoot."

Sydney fought the urge to smile, since it was apparent that Douglas Foster hadn't found any of it amusing, but she had to ask, "Was she the maid of honor?"

"God, no."

"Then who—"

"Everly," he interrupted. "Her last name was Everly. Kiki . . . no, that's wrong. Tiki Everly, that's it. How could I forget?"

"Tiki Everly," Sydney echoed, writing it down. "Is she a local?"

"I don't know that she's even from this planet," he said with a rueful laugh.

She drew a question mark after the name and underlined it; she was looking forward to interviewing Tiki. "Okay, now we're down to the last guest."

"The last . . . oh."

Years of listening for subtext, for what people meant but wouldn't say, had given her a heightened sensitivity to the tone of a person's voice. Instinctively, Sydney knew that for some reason, this guest was a sensitive issue with Foster.

"That would be Erin Cross," he said, squaring his shoulders. "Gary's date."

Seldom had she heard the word "date" spoken with such vehemence, the "t" enunciated with so much bite. "Am I right in assuming you didn't approve—"

"Of Erin? Not at all; she's a lovely girl. As it happens, she was Sean's girlfriend all through high school. After graduation, Erin enrolled at the university. Sean, of course, had the benefit of his trust fund, and was less concerned with pursuing a career. They drifted apart and eventually broke up—"

"Before Sean met Laura?"

"Long before. It was a mutual decision, and they remained friends. Regardless, it was totally inappropriate for Gary to have brought her."

"Why is that?"

"I may be old-fashioned, but I felt that it was rude and inconsiderate to say the least. Gary was the best man, but without consulting anyone, he decided to show up for the wedding with the groom's former sweetheart. It was a tactless, childish stunt."

"How did Sean react?"

Foster waved his hand dismissively. "He laughed it off, said Gary was just being Gary, doing his damnedest to stir things up. Sean was very forgiving of his friends, much more than I was."

"And Laura? How did she take it?"

"I honestly don't know. There wasn't a scene, if that's what you're asking."

But it might explain the dance with cousin Randy, Sydney thought. Perhaps Laura had not been amused by Gary's antics—nor by her betrothed's indulgence of his friend—and had resorted to a little payback.

An interesting possibility, but for now she continued with her original line of questioning. "All right then, what about Erin. Was she upset?"

"Again, I don't know." Foster ran his finger around the rim of his wine glass, and frowned. "I'm not an expert on female moods or behavior, Ms. Bryant. As a life-long bachelor, the feminine persuasion remains a mystery to me; I have never been able to look in a woman's eyes and tell what she's feeling."

"Not many men can."

"I can say, however, that I did not observe any overt hostility between Laura and Erin that afternoon. Nothing I personally saw or heard would lead me to believe there were hard feelings on either side."

Sydney nodded and made a note of that. "That covers the guest list, but what about the help?"

"My housekeeper was there throughout. Martha supervised the caterer's staff, but they simply served the food, cleaned up, and left."

"Is Martha still with you?"

This time when he smiled, there were laugh lines at the corners of his eyes. "Still and always. To be perfectly candid, I'd be lost without her. She is the one constant in my life."

Perhaps Martha could fill in the gaps, the hour that Foster had been absent. "Would it be possible to talk to her tonight?"

"As it happens, Wednesday is her day off. Will tomorrow do?"

"That'll be fine." Sydney tapped the pen on her notebook, running everything over in her mind. "Oh, and you mentioned music. Did you hire a band or—"

"Heavens, no. Alan has a recording studio here in town and he mastered a set of tapes of Sean and Laura's favorite songs as a wedding gift."

"A clever gift," she said.

"I think he still has them." His expression troubled, Foster looked down and then away. "Sean was in a hurry when the time came to leave."

"What time was that?"

"Five o'clock. They were driving up to Seattle for a two-week honeymoon, but planned to spend that first night in Mt. Shasta. I don't know how or why they ended up on that deserted road . . ."

Or who they met there, she thought. "How long did the party last after they left?"

"It didn't. Five minutes after they drove off, the house was empty, except for Martha and me." He grimaced and closed his eyes. "I remember being grateful for the peace and quiet. I didn't know then that the quiet would haunt me later."

"Quiet is good at that," Sydney said absently, thinking over the possibilities. A minute or two passed in silence, and then she closed her notebook. "One last question, if I may . . ."

"Certainly."

"Who do you think murdered your nephew and his wife?"

"Who do I think?" he repeated. "I . . . I have no idea."

"You never thought about who killed Laura if it wasn't Sean?"

"Well yes, I thought about it. I've always assumed it was a stranger."

Sydney met his questioning glance, and saw his expression change from dismay to something darker. Something very much like rage.

"Are you suggesting . . ."

"My guess is," she said evenly, "that the killer followed them from the reception that night."

Foster said nothing.

"I don't know why they were on that particular road, but it's clear that the car overheated; the vehicle impound record indicates the adjustable clamp connecting the hose to the radiator was loose—it takes a screwdriver to loosen it—and no doubt the car was leaking water from the time they pulled away."

"This is the first I've heard of it. You found this in a police report?"

"Yes, among other things."

"Go on."

"At some point, Sean realized they were stranded, that it wasn't simply a matter of letting the engine cool, that the radiator was bone dry and they needed water. So he set out on foot to get help."

"My God."

"Once Sean and Laura were separated," Sydney continued, "once he was too far away to protect her, it would have been a simple matter to—"

"—pick them off," Foster interrupted brusquely, "one at a time."

All she could do was nod; there was nothing left to say.

Five

While she was waiting for the valet to bring her car, Sydney watched Douglas Foster being assisted into a silver Mercedes limousine by the driver, a young black male with a body builder's physique, sporting a diamond stud in his left earlobe.

At street level of the parking structure, there was a certain amount of noise in the loading area—including the sound of passing traffic and a cacophony of squealing tires—but even so, it was possible to overhear the other patrons' conversations, echoing hollowly between the cement walls and pillars.

"Everything okay, Mr. Foster?" the driver asked, pausing before shutting the rear passenger door.

"Take me home," Foster ordered, staring straight ahead.

"Your wish is my command," he said good-naturedly, offering a half salute as he closed the door, then added, "so long as the check don't bounce." He effortlessly hefted the wheelchair into the open trunk, slammed the trunk lid, turned smartly to his left and trotted around the car to the driver's side.

The driver glanced her way, their eyes met, and Sydney smiled.

"Yo," he said, and winked. "Have a nice day."

"A little late for that," she said *sotto voce,* as the Probe appeared in the drive lane.

Ten seconds later, the limousine pulled away.

The streets of Reno were bumper-to-bumper with nostalgia buffs, cruising at roughly the speed of molasses in the dead of winter.

She didn't consider herself to be a car enthusiast, but even she was able to identify a red and white 1959 Corvette, and—thanks to a hint from its license plate—a 1932 Ford Roadster painted lemon-drop yellow.

There was music in the air, a medley of songs, from Dion's high energy "Runaround Sue" to a dreamy "Johnny Angel" to the yearning melody of "Do You Wanna Dance?" . . . and everything in between.

There were people out and about, walking from one casino to the next—now brightly lit in all their neon splendor—and indeed, many of the women were in fact wearing pastel poodle skirts. As for the men playing dress-up, most had reinvented themselves as greasers with slicked back hair, dressed in jeans with rolled cuffs and white T-shirts. A few wore leather jackets despite the heat.

Aside from the not infrequent beer belly and receding hairline, they might have been the reincarnation of The Wild Ones. Regardless, they looked as though they were having a good old time.

No harm in that, Sydney thought.

She took a wrong turn on her way back to the condo—one of the hazards of driving in an unfamiliar city after dark—but after twice pulling to the curb and consulting the map, she made it home.

This time she parked in the garage and went up the interior stairs to the private entrance. The action of the dead bolt was a little stiff; she had to pull the door to her to get the key to turn. Then, of course, the door wanted to stick.

Inside, the phone began ringing.

She gave the door a shove and it popped open just as the light from the automatic garage door opener blinked out. Yanking the keys from the lock, she located a switch and turned on the house lights, the better to see where she was going. Thankfully, there was a wall phone in the kitchen by the breakfast bar.

"Hello," she said, picking up on the third ring.

"Sydney?"

"Xavier, hi." Rather than sit on a bar stool, she boosted herself up onto the counter. There was something about being able to swing her legs freely as she talked that clarified her thinking.

"Where have you been? I've been trying to reach you all evening."

A glance at her watch revealed it was half past nine. "I had a dinner appointment with Douglas Foster," she said, and described in brief what she'd learned.

"So what do you think?"

"About Foster or the case?"

"Both."

She hesitated, considering. "You were right about Foster's determination to see his nephew's name cleared; he's in this for the duration."

"Didn't I tell you?"

"You told me. As for the case . . . I think you're right, and this wasn't an opportunistic murder—"

"Murders," her partner corrected.

"—or murders. It certainly wasn't coincidence that they wound up on that deserted road. Someone planned it. Someone in the wedding party."

"I always thought so," Xavier said, his tone uncharacteristically subdued. "Never could prove it, though."

"Who did you suspect?"

"All of them, in turn. But I wasn't actively working the case, so my involvement was peripheral at best. Which is why you need to talk to Jim Wagner."

"And he is?"

"An old buddy of mine from the department whose partner was the primary on the investigation. He put in his thirty a year or two back and is pulling down a pension now, but he still lives in the area."

"Is he willing to talk to me?" Ex-cops often had an us-versus-them mentality that followed them into retirement and frequently to the grave.

"More than willing; he's primed. Jim has an axe to grind with the department, so he's not entirely impartial. But if you take what he says with a grain of salt, you'll do fine."

"I can live with that. How do I reach him?"

"Got a pencil?"

Sydney retrieved the notepad and pen from her bag. "Ready," she said, and copied down the address and phone number. "Do you think he'd mind going with me out to the scene to have a look around?"

"Ask him. I'd be surprised if he said no; last time I talked to him he was pissing and moaning that all he ever does is watch TV and water the roses. Said he was turning into a frigging lawn ornament."

Sydney laughed. "Sounds like a touch of the retirement blues."

"Hell, I thought the hard-headed fool was a cement jockey all along."

"I'll give him your regards," she said diplomatically. "Is there anything else?"

"Actually, there is. I want you to have Jim lend you a gun while you're in town."

Taken aback, she didn't respond.

"I know what you're thinking," Xavier said in a rush. "What on earth has this jerk gotten me into—"

"Is there something you haven't told me?"

"No. Well . . . sort of, yes."

"Xavier . . ."

"Okay, okay. The thing is, there were a few, shall we say, *incidents* back in 1985 that were a little odd."

"Incidents?"

"Okay, threats."

"Threats."

"Actually, more like warnings."

Sydney sighed. "Spill it, Cochise. Who, what, where, when, and how."

"You forgot why."

"That too."

"All right. The who was yours truly—"

"Pardon me for interrupting, but why you if you weren't investigating the case?"

"Funny you should ask," Xavier said with a chuckle that sounded a little bit forced. "It's just that my picture was in the newspaper the next day, and then I accidentally ended up on the evening news. Twice."

"Accidentally?"

"It happens. I mean, the honchos were far too busy to play show-and-tell, so I graciously agreed to answer a few questions for a couple of reporters I owed favors to. I suppose somebody might have, you know, fixated on me because I was *visible*, there in the beginning."

"Maybe. Except—" she frowned "—if the killer was a member of the wedding party, you'd think he or she would know that you weren't the investigator . . . and then why would they target you?"

"Who the hell knows? Anyway, the what began with a note

stuck under the wiper on my patrol car while I was taking a dinner break one night, maybe a week after the murders."

"Takes nerve to leave a note on a cop car. What did it say?"

"Oh, it was vague, something like 'Butt out.' "

"Pithy," she said, "but nonspecific."

"Yep. But there was a follow-up message. It gets dusty patrolling those back roads, and a couple of days later someone wrote 'Mind your own damned business' in the dirt on the trunk—"

"Same handwriting?"

"I wasn't able to compare them, but it's possible. By the way, I took the first note to Property for safekeeping and they promptly lost the damned thing."

"Fingerprints?"

"Sydney honey," Xavier said. "You know real cops don't dust for prints at the drop of a hat. We wouldn't have time to do anything else."

"Granted, but it never hurts to ask." She hopped down from the counter and walked around the breakfast bar into the kitchen proper, where she opened the refrigerator, in search of a Pepsi or—she was desperate—even a Coke. The shelves were spotlessly clean and totally empty.

"Problem is," Xavier groused, "at that stage I wasn't sure what business I was minding that I shouldn't have been. It wasn't until the calls began that I knew the warnings were related to the Foster case."

There was, at least, ice in the freezer bucket. She opened a cabinet, found a glass and filled it with ice, then added water from the tap. She took a drink, savoring the cold as she swallowed, but missing the fizz. "Go on."

"Not much to tell. It started as hang-ups and progressed to what we out on the range would call 'a discouraging word.'

Nothing too extreme, mind you: 'Don't waste your time' or 'Sean killed her.' Silly stuff."

"Or downright stupid, maybe calling attention to yourself."

"That too. But you know how it is; you've had your share of anonymous calls . . ."

That was true, unfortunately. After Mitch separated from his wife eighteen months ago, Carol Travis had started calling her at the office and at home, more often than not hanging up without saying a word. Oddly enough, Carol had hired Xavier to watch her—as the alleged other woman—but he quickly determined that Carol's true motive was harassment, and he had resigned.

Shortly thereafter, Sydney had accepted his offer to pool their resources and talents, and *voilà*, Bryant & Walker Investigations was created.

"Point taken," she said, returning to the subject at hand. "Is there more to it? Shots fired?"

"Nothing that radical. But I was a police officer, and that fact alone may have kept it from turning nasty. And don't forget, Sean Foster was named in the media as a suspect, or actually, *the* suspect, early in the investigation."

"I don't know, Xavier. Adding everything up . . . a couple of phone calls, a vague warning or two . . . it doesn't amount to much."

"Maybe not. But remember, there's a killer out there who's gotten away with murder for fifteen years. You start asking questions and stirring things up again, he might get nervous. All I'm saying is be careful. Take precautions."

"Okay, I'll borrow a gun. Anything else?"

"Yeah, be sure to hook up the answering machine and fax. That way if you're out, I can leave word without wearing out the re-dial button on my phone."

"I have my laptop—"

"You know I don't trust e-mail. No telling who can access that . . ."

"—or I could rent a cell phone—"

"Sydney." He tsked again. "Might as well get a loud-speaker and *broadcast* to the world. Interception City, my dear."

She laughed. "A little phobic, aren't we?"

"Just cautious. Oh, and one other thing . . ."

"Yes?"

"Thank you."

"For what? I haven't done anything yet."

"This case is important to me, and you agreed to take it. I know you've got a lot of personal things going on, Mitch and . . . uh . . . it's inconvenient to work a case out of state . . . but you dropped everything to do this. I appreciate that."

"You'd do the same for me."

"As much as I'd like to think so, I wouldn't bet on it. Speaking of which . . . if you happen by one of the casinos, I'd be eternally grateful if you'd place a wager for me. I know the Super Bowl is a long way off, but—"

Sighing, she asked, "What team and for how much?"

Six

As a matter of self-preservation, the first thing Sydney did come morning was find the nearest store and stock up on Pepsi and the other essentials of life. Not that she had the slightest intention of cooking—and why should she, when Reno had more than its share of restaurants?—but if she felt like having a snack at midnight, at least the pantry wouldn't be bare.

She bought bread, peanut butter, blackberry preserves, whole-wheat crackers, Monterey Jack and sharp cheddar cheese, plus Red Flame seedless grapes, Gala apples from New Zealand, sweet Bing cherries, ripe summer plums, and a five-pound bag of navel oranges.

That seemed almost too virtuous, nutritionally speaking, so she added frozen mini-pizzas, a New York-style chocolate chip cheesecake, butter rum ice cream, and her favorite Mystic Mint cookies.

That done, she sat down with her notebook and began calling to schedule her appointments for the day. Her first call was to the Foster residence, and as expected, Martha answered the phone.

"Of course," Martha said when she'd introduced herself, "the mister told me you'd be calling. We've got a crew in today waxing and buffing the floors, and they're making an ungodly racket, but if you wouldn't mind chatting outside by the pool—"

"I think I can tough it out," Sydney said, tongue-in-cheek.

"Shall we make it eleven, then?"

"Fine," she agreed, and verified the directions to the house, in the southwest hills overlooking Reno, near Caughlin Ranch.

"I'll leave your name with the guard at the gate," Martha said in closing.

A guard at the gate, she thought, listening to the dial tone. The closest thing she had to a guard back home was a big black and white cat named Trouble, who incessantly roamed the apartment complex in search of cookies. But she supposed if a burglar happened to get between Trouble and his treat, blood might be shed.

"C'est la vie," she said, depressing the switch hook before dialing the next number on the partial list Douglas Foster had given her last night.

Thirty minutes later, she had left a message on Alan Foster's machine, gotten repeated busy signals for Erin Cross, and reached Jim Wagner to arrange a meeting at one. She also made courtesy calls to the Reno Police Department and the Washoe County Sheriff's office to advise them she was in from California to work a case in their bailiwick—not that they seemed terribly interested—and tracked down Gary West who, according to a former roommate, was currently living with his mother.

And evidently sleeping late.

"Shit, not that again," was West's yawning response when informed of the reason she was calling. Nevertheless he agreed, albeit without apparent enthusiasm, to a four o'clock appointment, and suggested they meet near the gift shop in the Peppermill casino. "If I'm not there, ask around. Everybody knows me at the Mill; there are a couple of dealers I can

just about claim as dependents on my fucking 1040. Someone'll point me out."

"I can hardly wait," Sydney said after hanging up the
phone.

Martha Barclay had the kind of face that looked as if she
had never frowned even once in her life. Her blue eyes twin-
kled with good humor, and she laughed easily and often. She
dimpled when she smiled, a hint of a blush complimenting
her creamy complexion. She, too, had that indulged, pampered look, which blurred the question of her age: she could
be in her late thirties—or early fifties.

Slender and petite at all of five feet tall, Martha was
graying prettily, her short dark hair frosted with white.
Dressed in a tailored navy blue shirtwaist, matching hose and
low-heeled shoes, she looked more like the lady of the house
than its keeper.

As for the house, it had an understated elegance that oh
so discreetly whispered wealth. The rooms were spacious,
with hardwood floors—in the process of being buffed to a
lustrous shine—and pristine ivory walls. The high ceilings
were inset with skylights, flooding the house with natural
light.

Foster's taste in art favored the geometric, with bold lines
and angles in black, blue and gray, with an occasional accent
of dark red.

The furnishings were modern in design, granite-topped
teak tables, the sofas and chairs upholstered in bluish-gray
Elmo leather that looked so meltingly soft, she couldn't resist
running her fingers across the back of a loveseat as they
passed by.

"I have to say, the mister is very pleased you're here, Ms.
Bryant," Martha said when they stepped out onto the wood

and brick deck which wrapped around three sides of the heptagonal house.

"Call me Sydney."

"Sydney then. The pool's this way."

The pool was below the deck, accessible by a ramp—for Foster's wheelchair—and two sets of wide, curving stairs. Surrounded by lush greenery and volcanic rock formations, the black-bottomed pool looked like a small lake, the water rippling in the brisk morning breeze.

There were several hammered glass tables at a distance from each other—presumably to allow for privacy—topped by green and beige canvas patio umbrellas, and circled by thick-cushioned chairs. Martha walked past the closest table to one nearest the waterfall that emptied into the dark depths of the pool.

"It's lovely here, don't you think?"

Sydney smiled, enjoying the feel of the wind in her hair. "I could get used to it."

"This is where I escape to when things get too hectic inside." She sat and promptly put her feet up on a second chair. "Do you mind?"

"Whatever makes you comfortable."

"That would take a hot bath, my terry cloth robe, and three fingers of brandy," Martha said and laughed. "But this will do in a pinch. Now . . . what can I do to help?"

"Actually, I want to talk to you about what happened at the reception during the time Mr. Foster was resting. Whatever you remember."

"As if I could forget. Sean was like a child on Christmas morning, just full of joy." The housekeeper's smile faded but did not disappear. "To die like that, within hours of what had to be the happiest moment of his life . . . the poor boy. And Laura, of course."

Interesting that Laura was an afterthought, Sydney noted. "Let's start with a little background. How long have you worked for Mr. Foster?"

"It'll be eighteen years in September. This was supposed to be a temporary job—I'd just gotten divorced and was planning to enroll at the university the following spring to finish my degree—but we hit it off so well that when the time came for me to apply for admission, Douglas offered me a rather stunning salary if I'd stay. Obviously, I did."

"Which would mean Sean was already an adult when you came to work here."

"Yes, he was twenty-one. But he and Alan were still living at home; it isn't easy to give all of this up, with or without a trust fund."

All of this, Sydney couldn't help but notice, was pretty damned impressive.

"That isn't the only reason they stayed," Martha went on. "Douglas did an excellent job raising them; when it was necessary, he disciplined with a fair and even hand. There was none of the competitive posturing that you might expect with three males under one roof."

"Not even when Sean showed an interest in Laura?" Sydney asked. "I understand Alan dated her first."

Martha nodded. "That was an awkward situation. Alan was quite taken with Laura; she was different from the other girls he'd gone out with. She was special, a lovely girl. He didn't talk about it—these aren't men who declare their intentions at the flutter of an eyelash—but a woman can always tell."

"Was he in love with her?"

"I thought so at the time."

"Have you changed your mind since?"

Martha shook her head. "Alan mourned for her. He was

devastated by all of it, the terrible accusations the police made about his brother, but it was plain that he cared deeply about Laura."

That did not eliminate him as a suspect, Sydney thought. Remorse and sorrow were closely related emotions, and it was difficult to distinguish one from the other. "What were his feelings toward Sean? Back when the police were issuing All Points Bulletins, did Alan believe his brother might be a killer?"

"Absolutely not."

"What did *you* think, in the beginning?"

"Me? Did I think Sean murdered . . . no. No. Not in the beginning, not ever."

The party line was holding firm. "If he didn't, who do you think did?" she asked, curious to see if Martha's answer would mirror that of her employer.

"Truthfully?"

Sydney couldn't help but smile. "I've always preferred the truth, yes."

"It's unkind of me, I'm sure, to accuse anyone without proof, but I remember wondering where Brad Goldwyn went after he left that evening."

"Goldwyn? What made you suspect him?"

Martha hesitated before answering, her gaze shifting to the dark waters of the pool. "You mentioned that you were interested in what happened while Douglas was napping. Well, the most vivid memory I have of that day—with the possible exception of that awful moment when the police showed up at the door—is of walking in on Laura and Brad Goldwyn."

That was a new twist, Sydney thought. "Walking in on them in what sense?"

"The usual one: they were kissing. At least, he was kissing her."

Sydney nodded to show she appreciated the distinction. "Was Laura resisting?"

"She seemed to be trying to push him away, her hands were on his chest like this—" Martha demonstrated, her hands flat, wrists bent, and elbows out "—but he wouldn't let her go."

"Did she cry out?"

"No. It wasn't . . . again, it's unkind of me to speak ill of the dead, but I didn't get the impression that she was struggling all that hard. She didn't kick at him, or really try to break free."

"Where were they?"

"In the guest suite, in the dressing room. Laura was in her slip; she'd gone to change her clothes before they left for the honeymoon—"

"And Goldwyn followed her," Sydney concluded. "What happened when they realized you were there?"

Martha looked scandalized. "He smirked at me! He had the nerve to claim he was simply kissing the bride, that she needed to be kissed by a real man since she'd just married a boy."

There had always been and probably always would be a certain percentage of men who equated masculinity with force. "How did Laura react?"

"She told him to go away, but she was . . . nonchalant. Even amused. I got the feeling that she wasn't really upset with him."

"Maybe it had happened before," Sydney said, thinking out loud, recalling what Douglas Foster had said about Laura being a flirt.

For the first time, Martha Barclay seemed genuinely troubled. "I have to say, there was a most peculiar *undercurrent* that afternoon. The dance—I know Douglas told you about

61

that—then Sean and Randy nearly coming to blows, and the kiss . . ."

All that and yet it didn't sound all that different from weddings she had attended over the years. There was an air of expectancy at a wedding, of changing loyalties and altered lives. Which perhaps explained her own reluctance to don a white gown and walk down that center aisle?

More than a little annoyed at the direction her thoughts were taking, Sydney wasted no time blocking that particular revelation from her mind, asking, "Is there anything else that struck you as odd? Tension between any of the other guests, or—"

"Not that I recall. I was busy most of the time, you understand. The caterer was having a problem with his vanilla sauce, which refused to thicken, so I gave him a hand in the kitchen. And Sean waited until absolutely the last minute to pack, at which point it became yet another crisis. He could be such a pain sometimes." Her smile was achingly sad. "We all miss him, even now."

"I can tell." Sydney closed her notebook. "I want to thank you for taking the time to meet with me. I appreciate your honesty."

"Will it help?"

It wasn't a question she could easily answer—there were far too many unknowns at present—but she saw the need in Martha's eyes to feel that her contribution mattered. "It all helps, one way or another."

Driving down the curved driveway, Sydney couldn't shake the feeling that this case was getting more complicated by the minute.

And the clock had been ticking for fifteen years.

Seven

Retired or not, Jim Wagner had the glint-eyed look of a frontier lawman. Six feet tall and as lean as a hard winter, he had short-cropped gray hair and a mustache that still bore traces of his redheaded youth. The sun had weathered his face with deep creases at his eyes and mouth, distinguished by an icy blue stare that would put the fear of God into any miscreant.

He also bore an uncanny resemblance to Sean Connery.

Be still my heart, Sydney thought as she walked up the three steps to where he stood waiting on the shaded porch of his ranch-style home.

"So you're the little gal who hitched up with Walker to play private eye," Wagner said, giving her the once-over after she introduced herself.

"I wouldn't put it quite that way, but yes, Xavier and I are partners."

Wagner grinned, tugging on his ear. "Well, he was a good cop back in the Dark Ages, and he's probably a passable snoop. He tells me that you're as smart as you are good looking . . . which is saying something."

"How you do go on," she said and laughed, feeling her color rise.

"I have my moments," Wagner said modestly. "Problem is, you're going to need every brain cell you can muster to crack the Foster case. It's a tough one."

"That's certainly the impression I'm getting. Xavier said you were one of the lead investigators?"

"Sad but true," he sighed. "Of course, Frank Micelli and I were like two mules pulling in opposite directions most of the time, and that didn't help."

"Micelli was the primary?"

"The primary pompous ass. But yeah, officially it was his case. We hadn't been partners more than a month when it went down. Turned out to be the first and last homicide we ever worked together."

"What happened?"

Wagner shrugged. "A personality conflict, as in he didn't have one, which I'll be the first to admit is not that uncommon. He liked calling the shots, got his kicks ordering everyone around. To which I took offense, and rightly, since he didn't have a clue."

"What did you—"

"Listen," Wagner interrupted, squinting at the sky, "if you want to take a look at the crime scene, we'd better head on out. Hot as it is, it's only gonna get hotter. We can talk on the drive over."

Sydney glanced over her shoulder at the Probe. "I've got air-conditioning—"

"Maybe so, but that itty bitty car of yours is too low to the ground to take us where we need to go."

"I thought the road was paved."

Wagner pulled a set of keys out of his pocket. "Sure is, where Laura Foster died, although it isn't what you'd call well-maintained. But I also want to show you where the boy's skull was found, and it's gonna take a four-wheel drive to get back in that canyon." He grinned again. "Besides, there's other ways to cool off."

★ ★ ★ ★ ★

Wagner drove a Jeep Wrangler that once upon a time might have been red. Minus doors and a top, it was disconcertingly . . . unenclosed. Looking at the road passing by in a blur, only feet from where she sat, Sydney recognized a heightened sense of vulnerability balanced by a quiet exhilaration at the lack of boundaries.

An interesting contradiction, she thought.

"So," Wagner yelled over the street noise, "what were you gonna ask me?"

"What? Oh, right. I just wondered if you agreed with Xavier that Sean Foster was innocent."

"Let's just say I kept an open mind. There were times I thought he probably did it. I mean, look how many women are killed by their husbands or boyfriends. But when he couldn't be found, it gave me pause."

"People do disappear," Sydney said, trying in vain to keep her hair out of her face. "Like that guy back east who murdered his entire family and then simply changed his name and started his life over—in Virginia, wasn't it?—pretty as you please."

"Oh it happens. This is a big country, with no lack of places to hide. But most of the time there's at least the beginning of a trail."

"There wasn't one?"

"None that we could find. Foster would have had to walk out of there, and we never found as much as a footprint cross-country. And if he had enough brass to stroll on down the road, a cruiser would've spotted him—"

"Unless he had someone pick him up."

Wagner slowed the Jeep as they neared the on-ramp to the 395, down-shifting smoothly. "I thought about that, but that would mean he was planning to kill her all along, and it just didn't have that feel."

"Did you have another suspect?"

"Not to speak of. Hold on," he said, and floored it, passing a furniture truck illegally on the right and then swerving in front of it before merging aggressively onto the freeway and into the fast lane, in the process narrowly missing a fin-tailed Cadillac convertible with a gold metal-flake paint job.

The Caddy driver, a woman wearing rhinestone-encrusted sunglasses, pink shorts, a white halter-top, and a pink scarf to keep her French twist in place, honked her horn furiously, gesturing in an unladylike manner.

Wagner ignored her.

The wind noise was far too loud to even attempt conversation, so Sydney settled back, gripping the side of the roll bar—which she hoped was an accessory and not a necessity—while reflecting on the tendency of ex-cops to drive like certifiable maniacs.

The high desert was beautiful in a stark, somewhat desolate way. The countryside had a windswept look, the low hills gently rounded, with sagebrush, wild heliotrope and Bluebunch wheatgrass hugging the slopes. Fences were few and far between, but those still standing collected tumbleweeds in a tangle, stopping their restless wandering.

The air was hot and dry, the wind stinging, blowing dust that had an alkaline taste.

They took a numbered exit off the highway, then turned left on a narrow road which ducked beneath the low overpass, heading west.

"Is this the road?" Sydney asked.

"Yes, ma'am." Wagner skirted a series of potholes that were a good eight inches deep. "There's not much traffic out here now, even less back then."

"Anyone live out here?"

"I think there might be a trailer or two tucked away in the hills. None within eyesight of the road, though, if you're wondering if anyone saw anything. The people who make this kind of an effort to get away from the city and other folks aren't inclined to wave at passersby from the stoop."

"That figures," Sydney said with a sigh.

"I told you, nothing about this case was easy." Driving slow now, to better avoid the canyonesque potholes, he came to a complete stop before crossing a rusting cattle catcher, the tires *thrumming* as they proceeded.

"I assume the road was in better condition then."

"Yeah, it was brand spanking new, which is why Walker was patrolling out here. There was some fool plan to build houses hereabouts, until reality set in and the developer cut his losses and bailed out."

"Reality as in . . ."

"There's no water in the ground to drill wells, and it's too far from the city to run water lines, unless you have unlimited access to Fort Knox."

"How does anyone survive?"

"They have private tanks, truck the water in from town, but I doubt Foster would have known that. I don't imagine that any of these desert rats would have given him any water if he'd gotten down on his knees and begged."

"That doesn't seem neighborly."

"No, but they don't exactly give a rat's ass. No one moves out here to polish their social skills. And water is just too precious to waste on a stranger, particularly in the summer."

"So—" she looked around "—why pull off here, in the middle of nowhere? There isn't even any shade to speak of. Why not stay along the highway?"

"Bad luck, I guess. His car overheated. This was a freshly paved road, and there were, you know, those bright-colored banners developers like to use to lure potential buyers to the property site."

"So he thought he could get help. And thought wrong."

"That's how I figure it."

They were approaching a bend in the road, where it curved to the south, and Sydney heard Xavier's voice in her mind: *I saw a Mustang parked there with the hood up, radiator steaming, and both doors standing wide open . . . don't ask me why or how, but when I saw that, I knew there was trouble.*

In spite of the heat, she shivered.

"This is it," Wagner said, just beyond the bend as the Jeep coasted to a stop.

There wasn't much of anything to see, but Sydney walked along the road, getting a feel for the place. Shading her eyes from the afternoon sun, she was unable to spot anything that remotely resembled a house or trailer in any direction.

The highway was no longer in view, nor could she hear the drone of traffic even though they were probably less than two miles away from it.

She'd expected sounds to carry better out here.

A jack rabbit darted across the road a hundred yards further on to the west. That and a lazily circling hawk were the only visible signs of life.

"What do you think?" Wagner asked, coming up to stand beside her in the center of the road.

"I think it's a lonely place to die."

"I don't know," Wagner said, squinting up at the sky. "I'd rather have this be the last thing I see than a ceiling in a hospital room."

She couldn't resist looking up at that vibrant blue sky again, with the feel of the sun on her face. The warm wind ruffled her hair and dried the sweat on her brow. "It is peaceful out here."

"But I know what you're saying. A woman alone in an isolated spot like this, with nowhere to run, nowhere to hide . . ."

"Can you show me where they found her?"

"Follow me."

It wasn't far. As Xavier had described, there was a cluster of sagebrush approximately fifty yards off the right shoulder. There was a slight rise to the land, but not enough to give cover to the killer, who'd stabbed Laura Foster to death in plain view of the road . . . if there'd been anyone to witness it.

"Here," Wagner said, a moment later.

Perhaps it was her imagination, but Sydney felt a chill in the air as she stood near the place where Laura had died, her life's blood soaking into the hard-packed earth.

"You've seen the crime scene photos, haven't you?"

Sydney nodded, then sat on her heels, placing her hand flat on the ground. She felt an overwhelming sadness, at the loss of a young life, the silencing of laughter, of all that might have been.

A minute passed, or maybe five, and then she stood, not bothering to brush the dirt from her hand. "Take me to where they found Sean."

"You got it," Wagner said.

Eight

Wagner drove to where the road ended in a paved turnout, another two or three miles west of the highway. There was a slight rise of elevation, and when Sydney looked behind her, she could see 395 in the distance, shimmering in the heat of day.

"This'll just take a second," Wagner said, killing the engine. He hopped out of the Jeep to loosen the hubs on the front wheels, grunting with the effort.

"From up here," she said, thinking aloud, "someone could easily have seen their car stranded by the side of the road."

"Absolutely." Wagner went around to the back of the Jeep and rummaged under the tarp that covered the cargo area. He pulled out a gallon-sized water container and brought it to her. "We're about to raise a ton of dust, so you'd best wet your whistle now. Sorry I don't have a cup or anything; I usually drink from the bottle."

"This is fine." She unscrewed the cap and drank the tepid water gratefully, then handed it back to him. "Am I correct in assuming that the police had a look around up here?"

"As a matter of fact, I did it myself," Wagner said, then tilted his head back and drank with apparent abandon, little rivulets of water running down his neck. When he had finished, he wiped his mouth with the back of his arm. "It was dark before I got the chance, but I walked the turnout with my flashlight."

"Find anything?"

"Like tire tracks, you mean?" he asked, feigning wide-eyed innocence.

Sydney returned the look, aware that he was yanking her chain. "What I had in mind was a signed confession from the killer."

"Or maybe a bloody glove, you think?" He grinned. "That would be nice, wouldn't it? It'd take a real stupid killer . . . although you know what they say about stupidity? Stupidity is—"

"—job security for cops."

"You got it. But joking aside, there were all kinds of tire tracks going off-road. Far too many to single out any one set."

"Why am I not surprised?"

"Hey, you're catching on." Wagner hesitated, his expression turning serious. "A homicide case is never a cake walk, and even though he may have set a world record for jumping to the wrong conclusion, Micelli wasn't totally incompetent. We might have missed something, but it wasn't for lack of trying. It almost never is."

They drove into the low brown hills that seemed to undulate from the mountains to the west. Wagner took care to avoid the clusters of sagebrush and Russian thistle—the precursor to tumbleweed—but judging by the crushed remains of many of the plants, not everyone did.

Now and again they came upon an outcropping of rocks on which some half-wit had spray-painted a message for the ages, pearls of adolescent wisdom as in "Deadhead Forever," "Party On" and "Cocaine Rules."

Beside her, Wagner made a derisive sound. "Are you enjoying the scenic wonders of northern Nevada, courtesy of the off-road tagging crew?"

"It's hardly the petroglyphs," Sydney noted.

"No, but it might be scientific proof that Neanderthals still exist."

She smiled and looked away, scanning the horizon where thunderhead clouds were forming. "We already have plenty of circumstantial evidence that they do . . . and the primitive mind-set is catching."

"Amen to that," Wagner said, his voice gruff, "and heaven help us all."

"This is it." Wagner parked near the entrance to a gully that wound between a trio of gently rolling hills, angling the Jeep so that the cloud of trailing dust floated by, missing them entirely.

Sydney noticed yellow markers on either side of the gully, lengths of crime scene tape which had been tied on the underbrush to identify the spot. There were plenty of tire tracks as well, some of which had obviously been made in mud, long since dried.

"We'll have to walk from here," Wagner said in the sudden silence after he shut the engine off. He reached across her, taking a heavy-duty flashlight from the map box and turning it on, shining the beam at close distance on his hand to test it. "Even in mid-day it's pretty dark back in there."

"How far is it?"

"About a quarter of a mile. Come on."

Sydney got out of the Jeep and followed Wagner as he led the way into the narrow canyon. "Was the site secured?" she asked.

"Well yeah, initially. Anytime someone finds human remains, the first order of business is containment of the scene, followed by a thorough search of the surrounding area. They spent two or three days out here with metal detectors, sifting dirt, and scouring every square inch of the place."

"Did they find anything? Bullet fragments or a wedding ring?"

"No. The truth of the matter is, no one is a hundred percent certain that this is even a crime scene. The jaw was missing, and the skull might have rolled for miles in one of the gully-washers we had last winter."

It was a gruesome image, a human skull being swept downstream by a torrent of water, turning over and over, the eye sockets empty and sightless, silt collecting in the cranial vault until finally it was too heavy to be carried further . . .

Sydney made her own effort at containment, blocking that mental picture from her mind. Quickening her steps to keep up with Wagner's longer stride, she asked, "Who found the . . . remains?"

"A rock hound, I think. You gotta feel for the guy; here he is, out on a lazy Sunday afternoon, out looking for geodes or whatever, and instead he stumbles upon a skull."

"Did he move it or—"

"Nope, didn't touch it. He hiked back to his truck and used his cellular phone to call the Sheriff's Department and, coincidentally, a local television station where his sister works."

"Did the story get a lot of media play?"

Wagner shrugged. "About average. The past six months or so there have been a fair number of skeletal remains discovered. A couple out in Verdi, another near Cold Springs if I remember right."

Taking belated notice of how isolated the canyon was— and how chill the air out of the direct sunlight—Sydney rubbed her bare arms. "This would be an ideal place to dump a body."

"One of many," Wagner said, turning on the flashlight and directing it in a sweep in front of them. "Watch your footing through here."

There was an accumulation of rocks behind a twisted branch that evidently had been washed down the gully in the rains, since there were no trees nearby. Considering what had brought them here this afternoon, she couldn't help but look at the jumble of rocks and wonder if all were what they seemed.

Stepping carefully, she crossed the rock pile, steadfastly avoiding any bone-colored stones. The click of the rocks shifting beneath her feet was an eerie counterpoint to the sound of her pulse in her ears.

Out of the corner of her eye, she saw what looked like a human vertebrae. On closer examination it proved to be a gnarled section of the branch.

A few minutes later, back on level ground, Wagner stopped. "I can't pinpoint the exact spot, but it was in this vicinity." He shone the light on where an X had been chalked on a four-foot high boulder—not far from yet another missive from a spray paint wordsmith parroting Charlie Manson's "Helter Skelter"—and then down at the gully floor.

There were signs that the earth had been disturbed, dug up and sifted, as Wagner had said. Clumps of silt formed odd mounds that would last until the first hard rain sent water flowing down the hills and through the canyons, seeking the low ground.

As she had before, Sydney bent down and touched the dirt, feeling its cool silkiness beneath the palm of her hand. It was her own way of paying her respects to Sean Foster, as she had Laura.

"Has anyone an idea of where Sean was shot, if it wasn't here?"

Wagner frowned, shaking his head. "I'm not exactly in the loop, you know. But realistically, it could be anywhere. One mile or ten, up in these hills . . . or a hundred yards from where we're standing."

Like a needle in a haystack, she thought.

"If you want to, we can walk further on."

"I want to." Sydney straightened, but took only a single step before hesitating. "Jim, tell me something. If the prevailing theory is that Sean took his own life, what about the gun? They didn't find the gun."

"Not to my knowledge."

"Then where is it?" Sydney frowned. "For that matter, where is the knife that Laura was stabbed with? If he did it."

"Presumably with the rest of the bones. Wherever the hell they are."

"But a heavy object like a gun or a knife should be relatively easy to find. You said they used a metal detector . . . how large of an area did they search?"

"That I don't know. The thing is, they didn't have a positive ID in the beginning, so they probably weren't even looking for the gun or a knife. And as I said, nobody in the department is claiming this is where Sean was shot, by his own hand or otherwise."

Of course he was right, but still . . . if the killer had been clever enough to make it appear that Sean had murdered Laura, might not he or she have purposefully left both of the weapons with Sean's body, assuming that he would eventually be found?

Even if she unearthed either weapon, there was only a slim chance that it could be traced back to the killer—knives were notoriously difficult to trace—but a slim chance was far better than none. And if nothing else, the discovery of one or both instruments of murder all these years later might seriously disturb the killer's peace of mind.

And a disturbed killer might make mistakes.

To that end she asked, "Can you find out the boundary of the search area?"

Wagner scratched his head doubtfully. "I suppose I could, but how would that help?"

"I don't know that it would, necessarily," she admitted, "but at this stage, I want to gather as much information as I possibly can."

"You aren't planning to come back out here on your own, are you? Because I have to tell you, the desert is no place for a woman alone."

"Don't worry," Sydney said, avoiding his eye. "I'm not that reckless."

His expression was skeptical. "That isn't what Xavier says."

On the slow, bumpy drive to the paved road, Sydney took pains to identify a few distinctive features of the landscape so that if she had to, she could find her way back. In particular she noted a cluster of Snakeweed, its tiny yellow blossoms a vivid contrast to the muted brown and green background.

She would need to rent a four-wheel drive vehicle and a metal detector, but—

"Wait a minute," she said as a thought occurred to her. "Assuming that Sean was taken further off-road before he was shot, wouldn't the killer have to have been driving a four-by-four?"

Wagner groaned. "Don't ask me to remember who was driving what, because I can't tell you. It wasn't an element of the case."

"There would still be records, wouldn't there? At the DMV?"

"I am not privy to the inner workings of the DMV," he said archly. "Furthermore, even if they do have registration records from 1985, I wouldn't care to be the one requesting them."

"Why is that?"

"Because it would probably take another fifteen years to get 'em. I don't mean to bad-mouth the efficiency of state workers, but there are glaciers that move faster and have a warmer temperament."

Sydney laughed. "Then what do you suggest?"

Wagner glanced at her sideways. "Listen to your instincts. Someone had a reason for wanting those two young kids dead. That's what *we* missed the first time around, a motive."

"I know you're right—"

"Damned straight I am. Besides, most everybody I knew back then had access to an off-road vehicle, including the X-man. They're as common as ticks."

Grabbing ahold of the roll bar as the Jeep drove down a steep and rocky incline, Sydney could understand why.

Back at Wagner's, she waited on the porch while he went inside to get the gun he was lending her at Xavier's request. It was almost four o'clock—they'd spent over two hours in the desert—and she had to wonder if Gary West would wait for her if she showed up late. She considered calling and asking to have him paged at the casino, but decided against it.

West had admitted to being a gambler. More than likely he'd amuse himself at the tables.

Sydney hadn't much experience with casinos beyond a couple of weekend trips to Las Vegas with a friend from college after she'd turned twenty-one, but she still recalled the sense she had being there, of distorted time . . . or rather of timelessness.

Lulled by the subdued lighting and the near constant clatter of coins dropping into the slot machine trays, it was deceptively easy to lose track of the hour. She remembered walking out of Caesar's Palace once and being startled to discover that night had fallen, that she'd idled away an entire afternoon.

Behind her, the screen door creaked. "Here you go," Wagner said, handing her a blue zippered gun case and a box of .38 ammunition. "You should know that in Nevada, you can keep a loaded weapon under the front seat of your car or in the glove compartment, but you can't carry it concealed on your person without a permit."

"Thanks for the warning."

"Of course, the sheriff's been passing out carry permits like lollipops on Halloween since the restrictions were eased a few years ago. Not that restrictions ever stop some folks from packing. So watch yourself, young lady."

"Another victory for the NRA," she noted.

"Me, I'm still pulling for the right to arm bears. As for that—" he nodded at the gun "—I hope to hell you don't need it."

So did she.

Nine

Gary West had not been exaggerating when he'd said they knew him at the Peppermill casino.

"Gary?" the clerk at the information desk said without the slightest hesitation. "I saw him a few minutes ago. You might check the pit—"

"Excuse me?"

"It's where the table games are. Gary's favorite blackjack dealer is working today, I know. I'd try the pit first, or maybe the sports book."

Sydney smiled and shook her head. "It would help if I knew what he looked like; I've never met the man. Could you describe him for me?"

The clerk, whose name tag identified her as Betsy, smiled back, dimpling prettily. Betsy's earrings sported miniature dice that dangled in endless combinations, both winning and losing numbers. "He is *so* cute. Gary's like, five foot eight, slim but not skinny, and he's got a great little behind—"

Which was more than Sydney wanted to know.

"—he has curly brown hair and brown puppy dog eyes. When he looks at me with those big sad eyes, I just want to . . . ooh!"

Definitely more than she wanted to know. "What's he wearing? I mean, if he's sitting down or something and I can't check out his tush."

"A Hawaiian shirt, of course. I'm pretty sure it's black with orchids on it; black is *his* color, and don't think he doesn't know it. Men are every bit as vain as women are, don't you agree?"

"It depends—"

"They are, take my word for it." Betsy, who looked to be all of twenty-one, sighed as though that had been a hard-learned lesson. "Anyway, he's usually in Levi's and, of course, cowboy boots."

Sydney thanked her, then went off in search of puppy dog eyes.

Gary West was relatively easy to spot amid the Fifties celebrants and business-suited gamblers that crowded the casino floor. He was indeed at a blackjack table, at the blonde dealer's extreme left, and had a stack of red five-dollar chips riding on his hand.

Not wishing to interrupt in the middle of the game, Sydney stood back and watched.

There were four other players at the table, one of them a woman who looked to be in her seventies, who evidently was slowing the game by her indecisive play.

"Now don't rush me," the woman fretted. "I know I'm supposed to stand on fifteen, but every time I do, I wind up losing—"

"In my lifetime, would you please?" snarled the man at her left, puffing furiously on his cigar. "It's a frigging three-dollar bet!"

The blonde dealer frowned disapprovingly at the man but remained silent, waiting patiently for the old woman to make up her mind.

The woman's hands shook slightly, from palsy or perhaps nervousness. "I just don't know."

"For crying out loud," the cigar smoker erupted, "take a hit or don't, but do something before the rest of us get senile too."

"There's no call for that," Gary West said, leaning forward to look directly at the man. "If you aren't happy with the play at this table, maybe you'd better take your game elsewhere."

Like a lot of bullies, this one deflated instantly when challenged. "Sorry, I didn't mean anything by it . . . it's been a long day."

"I'm not the person you need to apologize to," West said pointedly.

The man muttered an apology to the old woman. Perhaps emboldened by West's gallantry, she decided to take a hit and drew a six, making twenty-one. Beside her, the cigar smoker busted after hitting a twelve.

West stood on seventeen. The dealer hit a sixteen with a queen, also busting, which meant that everyone except the cigar smoker had won.

Sydney was moderately impressed. She waited until the bets had been paid and then stepped forward to introduce herself to Gary West.

Cocker spaniel eyes, she thought illogically when he turned to look at her.

"You're a private investigator?"

"Yes. I'm sorry I'm late."

"I hadn't noticed." West stood up, slid five red chips across the felt to the dealer as a tip, and nodded a farewell to the old lady, whose gratitude lit up her face. "Have a good one, darlin'."

"Later," the blonde dealer said, already pitching the next hand.

"Where can we talk?" Sydney asked, following him as he

wove his way through the seemingly continuous rows of video slot machines, most of which were in play. The machines, she noticed, made an automated sound of approval—not unlike the way the Tribbles used to purr at Captain Kirk—when coins were fed into them.

West glanced over his shoulder at her. "You mind an early dinner?"

"That'll be fine." Which was an understatement: she hadn't eaten since this morning, and that didn't qualify as breakfast, consisting of nothing more substantial than a Pepsi, half an orange, and a handful of grapes.

The Island Buffet was resplendent with a riot of artificial plants, from exotic ferns to palm trees. There were mirrors everywhere, and glass columns filled with marine plants in a current of bubbling water. Blue tube lighting lined the silver metal ceiling, creating the illusion of an undersea glow.

The buffet had just begun the dinner service, and after a quick circuit of the tables, Sydney slid into the dark green leather booth. While waiting for West to join her, she took note of a boisterous party of five poodle-skirted women of her mother's age who were being led to a booth across the aisle.

Chuck Berry's raucous "Johnny B. Goode" was playing somewhere in the casino, loud enough to be heard throughout the restaurant.

The women were laughing so hard that several of them had tears running down their rouged cheeks. As the dazed hostess stood by, a rather plump lady did an impromptu little dance that sent her skirt twirling above her waist, revealing red silk panties.

The members of her party cheered, and many of the other patrons whistled and clapped.

Sydney joined in the applause just as Gary West returned

to their booth carrying two heaping plates of food, one hot, the other cold.

"I haven't done anything yet," West said humbly, "but I never say no to an ovation, so thank you very much. Has the cocktail waitress come by?"

"Not yet."

"Shit. I'm dry enough to spontaneously combust and there's no one to take a drink order."

"In that case—" Sydney pushed a goblet brimming with ice water across the table to him.

"Never touch the stuff," he said with a shudder, "although if I burst into flames, I'd appreciate it if you'd use it to put me out."

Sydney smiled, sensing that he was ill at ease with her, or more probably, with the reason she had for being here. "My pleasure. In the meantime, I have a few questions . . ."

West speared a baby corn with his fork and frowned. His demeanor changed abruptly, from flippant to sullen, his shoulders slumping as though he was carrying the weight of the world upon them. He hesitated, stuffed the tiny cob in his mouth whole, chewed once and then said around it, "Yeah, sure. Whatever."

So he was less than enthused at the prospect of playing Q & A. Not a surprise. "When did you first meet Sean?" she asked in her very best non-confrontational manner.

"In the third grade. He picked me for his kickball team, and I—" West smiled thinly "—I was eternally grateful for that. I was nine, a year older than the others, but I was still the shortest boy in class, a scrawny little knock-kneed runt. Some little kids are fast, but not me, so I was always the last one chosen. Always the last kid, standing on the side-lines . . ."

Seeing the distant look in his eyes, she marveled at the

ability of childhood traumas to inflict pain that could linger for a lifetime.

"But Sean picked me before any of the kids who could run fast or kick straight. And nobody dared to say a mean word about it. Nobody even laughed."

"You were friends after that?"

"We were best friends. Of course, I nearly got creamed playing kickball that day and we got our butts royally whipped by the other team, but all Sean said to me afterwards was 'Good game.' "

"Was Sean popular in school?"

West nodded. "Everybody liked him, including the teachers. He was intelligent, but not an egghead; he never rubbed it in that he was smarter than you. And everyone knew about his parents getting killed."

Sean would have been seven and more than likely in second grade when he was orphaned in 1968.

"Not," West added quickly, "that people were feeling sorry for him. I mean, they did, but sympathy wasn't the reason they liked him. He was friendly and funny in his own twisted way. He was always respectful to adults, which was probably why the teacher appointed him team captain in the first place."

"Sounds like a nice kid."

"Nice and genuine. Anyway, Sean and I were tight, like brothers. We went all the way through high school together. Reno was a small town back then, and there wasn't much else to do other than hang out. There were various, well, I guess you'd call them cliques."

"Was Erin Cross in your clique?"

"Yeah, she was." West raised a hand, signaling to the long-legged cocktail waitress who was making the rounds. "Do you want a glass of wine?"

Why was it men assumed that all women liked wine? Personally, she'd prefer molten lava over Chablis any day. "I'll pass. Alcohol goes straight to my head—"

"That's exactly why I drink," he said with an impish grin, "to get toasted."

The cocktail waitress came over to their table. Dressed alluringly in a French-cut outfit with a red sequined vest, matching choker, and black tails that only just covered her assets, she smiled fondly at Gary West. "What'll it be, love? The usual?"

"Gin and tonic, and make it quick." He clasped both hands to his throat and spoke in a choked whisper. "I'm about to die of dehydration."

"I wondered why the buzzards were circling overhead," the waitress teased. "And for you, Miss?"

Sydney shook her head. "Nothing, thanks."

"Oh oh, Gary," the waitress said, and winked. "Looks like someone's losing his touch."

"Sorry about that," he said when the waitress had gone. "Claudia likes to give me a bad time because I turned forty this year and I'm single."

"You've never been married?"

"Never have been, never will be." He shelled a shrimp and dabbed it in sauce. "Marriage has never appealed to me. Evidently, I don't have the genetic make-up for it. It's chromosomal."

She couldn't help but wonder if Gary West had been on the long list of Laura's admirers. For now, she settled for returning to the business at hand: "You were going to tell me about Erin."

"Was I?"

"Specifically, I wanted to ask why you took Erin to Sean and Laura's wedding."

A flicker of irritation showed in his eyes. "Why not? I mean, she and Sean were okay after they stopped seeing each other."

"Douglas Foster is of the opinion that you were trying to stir things up," she said. "That perhaps you were hoping to cause a little trouble."

"He would think that," West said bitterly.

"Is he wrong?"

"Yes, he's wrong. Look—" he leaned forward, bracing his elbows on the table "—it might not have been the best idea, but nothing came of it. It's not like there was a cat fight or anything."

"You haven't answered my question," Sydney said, cutting him off in mid-rationalization. "Whatever ultimately came of it is secondary to your intent. Why did you bring Erin to Sean's wedding?"

West didn't answer immediately. Jaw clenched, he stared at her for a full minute, as if expecting her to back down.

She didn't blink.

"All right, fine," he said with a sigh. "I'm not proud of it, but I was young then—"

Youth, she thought, the perennial get-out-of-jail-free card.

"—and if you have to know, I'll tell you. Sean wanted me to be his best man. Laura objected. She thought Alan should do it."

"What's wrong with that? They were brothers."

"And blood is thicker than water, yeah I've heard that shit a million times before."

Sydney heard the anger in his voice . . . and something more. Something she couldn't yet define. "That made you mad enough to risk ruining the wedding?"

"Oh, give it a rest. The damned wedding wasn't ruined, so where's the harm?"

"And you were the best man," she shot back, "so what was your problem?"

"First of all, Sean had already asked me. If he'd wanted Alan to stand up with him, he would have asked Alan to start with."

This was, Sydney realized, very much about choosing sides. Grade school stuff. Then again, she could empathize with him to a certain degree. He and Sean were longtime friends, and Laura was an outsider who threatened to come between them. "You brought Erin to get even?"

"More or less. The truth is, I knew Laura suggested Alan because that was more dramatic. She was desperate to be an actress, you know, and she was forever arranging these little *scenes*. Having a former lover standing next to Sean, lusting after her as she married him would be a show-stopper. She got off on that kind of thing."

"I wasn't aware that Alan had been Laura's lover."

"Take it from me, they slept together. Laura wasn't the type of girl who spent a lot of time saying 'no'. Everybody knew it, too. So I figured, hey, if she wants drama and unrequited love, I'll give it to her . . . in spades."

Sydney took that as an indication that Gary West wasn't a dues-paying member of the Laura Foster fan club. "Was Erin in on your plan?"

His drink arrived just then—saved by the bell?—and he all but inhaled it. Claudia had brought a second drink, which she placed on a napkin in front of him. "Slow down, love," she cautioned, "the night is young."

"But as you're forever telling me," West said when he came up for air, "I'm not."

Claudia gave Sydney a sympathetic look. "So it's Mr. Hyde tonight, eh?"

West's only response was to hand the cocktail waitress a

twenty-dollar bill. "Keep the change."

When they were alone, Sydney asked again, "Was Erin in on the plan?"

"No, she was not. As a matter of fact, she was pissed off at me when she found out that Sean hadn't known she was coming. She barely spoke to me all afternoon, and wouldn't let me drive her home."

"How did she—"

"A cab," he said. "And she left early, about four-thirty."

Sydney had given a fair amount of thought as to how best to raise the subject of cars, as in who owned or had access to a four-wheel-drive vehicle. Unfortunately, she hadn't been able to devise a subtle approach, and decided for the sake of expediency to be direct. "What kind of car were you driving back then?"

Reaching for his drink, West hesitated, his eyes meeting hers. "Why do you ask?"

"I think that should be obvious." Being out in the sun had given her a slight headache, and she wasn't in the mood for mind games. It was time, she thought, to bluff. "I can always check with the DMV, but unless you have something to hide . . ."

"I had an MGB-GT. A little two-seater. British racing green, if you're interested. I still have it, in fact. It's parked in my mother's garage." He tossed back his second gin and looked at her with his eyelids at half-mast. "You know it's unhealthy the way Uncle Dougie keeps obsessing about Sean and Laura. It's sick, really."

Uncle Dougie? Without question, the booze had kicked in. "You're over it then?" she asked.

"Hell, yes. Grief is wasted on the dead. No matter how hard you wish it, no one ever comes back."

"True, but—"

"Someone dies, you gotta get on with your life, or you might as well be buried with 'em." West grimaced, pinching the bridge of his nose with his thumb and forefinger. "Are we about done here?"

"Not quite. Martha Barclay said you took Sean outside after he and Randy got into it that night."

"Who said?"

"The housekeeper, Martha."

"Oh, right, I remember her." He picked the twist of lime from his empty glass and sucked on it, trying to get every last drop of gin. "She told you what?"

"That you talked with Sean privately after he got upset over the way his cousin was dancing."

"Another of Laura's little scenes," West said, frowning. "An encore."

"Is that what you and Sean talked about?"

"Hardly; we had more important things to discuss than her performances."

"Such as?"

"I told him I'd set up an appointment with the bank for the Monday after he was due back from the honeymoon, and that I would have our business plan done by then."

"You were going into business together?"

"Yep."

This was the first she'd heard of a joint venture involving Sean. That surprised her, since it would seem to be the type of detail Douglas Foster would have mentioned . . . that is, if he knew of his nephew's plans. "What kind of a business?"

Gary West grinned. "We were going to open a health resort."

"Do you mean a spa? Like the Golden Door?"

"Only better. It was very high concept—I'm good at formulating top-end, ritzy stuff—and we'd been talking about it for years, since high school." His grin faded. "Finally, it was going to happen . . . a dream come true."

Sydney regarded him curiously. "And then Sean disappeared."

West nodded.

"You must have been devastated."

He took a deep breath, released it, then met her eyes. "You have no idea."

"All right, last question. Where did you go that evening after the reception?"

"Where else would I go? I hit the casinos."

"I take it you went to more than one?" she asked, knowing it would be difficult if not impossible to verify his whereabouts.

"Hey, the night was young and so was I . . . and I thought I was going to be rich."

"Did you see anyone you knew?"

"Shit, when the dice are hot, everyone's your friend. It's only when you're down that people look right through you. Whether anyone would remember me or not, I can't say, but I kind of doubt it."

"Were you winning that night?"

"Oh yeah." His smile was cryptic, not reaching his eyes. "I couldn't lose."

Ten

On her way out, she detoured to the sports book and placed Xavier's bets; fifty dollars on the San Diego Chargers—which he called his 'loyalty long-shot'—and another fifty on the Baltimore Ravens. Pocketing the tickets, she walked out through the maze of slot machines and wondered at the rapt concentration of the gamblers, staring at an endless variety of video screens.

Sydney had left the air conditioner on low at the condo all day, and when she got back from the casino at eight o'clock, the cool silence was a welcome relief from the ninety-plus degree weather.

Dry heat was still heat, after all.

She went directly upstairs to take a shower, even though she had calls to make to arrange her appointments for tomorrow. Standing under a fine spray of lukewarm water, she washed off what felt like an inch of dust and luxuriated in the silky feel of soap on her skin, tender from exposure to the high altitude sun.

Afterwards, wrapped in a towel, she paused in front of the French doors that opened onto the master bedroom's balcony just as the city streetlights began to flicker on below. The casinos were already displaying their neon flash and dazzle, with hot pinks and deep purple predominating.

In the far distance, a siren wailed, a plaintive reminder of the random nature of life . . . and of death. Not that she needed reminding.

After drying off, she dressed in a T-shirt and cut-off jeans, then went barefoot down to the kitchen for an ice cold Pepsi, AKA the nectar of the gods.

She went next to the living room where she had set up the fax and answering machine. There was a single fax from her office, a handwritten note from Xavier that included an address and phone number in Lake Tahoe for Brad Goldwyn that she'd requested this morning.

"Nothing yet on Tiki Everly" the note read. "Experian has never heard of her, but I'll pursue this to the ends of the earth."

There were five messages on the answering machine, two from Hannah at the office, and one each from her mother, Mitch and, surprisingly, Ethan. As a dutiful daughter, she called her mother first.

There was also the little matter of her not having told her mother about this trip beforehand. She'd meant to swing by her mother's house on the way to the airport yesterday, but there'd been so much to do, she had simply run out of time.

Guilt was a prime motivator, as always.

"Sydney," Kathryn said, "what in heaven's name are you doing in Reno?"

"Working a case."

"Yes, well, that was a silly question, wasn't it? Work is all you ever do, dear."

Sydney sat on the wooden arm of the futon. "Mom . . . I thought you agreed not to criticize my work habits—"

"I don't mean to be critical, honey. It was merely an observation."

It was merely an observation in the same way that a tornado was merely wind, she thought. "Okay, if you say so."

"I do. Are you there alone?"

"Of course I'm alone." Sydney frowned. "Why wouldn't I be alone?"

"Never mind. When will you be home?"

"I'm not sure." Changing the phone to her left hand, she reached down to massage her right calf, which was sore from all of the hiking she'd done. "A week to ten days I'd guess."

"That long?"

"It could be, I don't know. I've barely scratched the surface of the case."

"I don't suppose—" long distance amplified Kathryn's sigh "—that there's any point in asking if you might come home for the weekend."

"Probably not. Why? Is something going on?" She was usually pretty good at keeping family obligations in her head, but her life had been spinning at roughly a thousand revolutions per minute these past few weeks, and it was well within the realm of possibility that she might have forgotten a promise made months ago for a Saturday barbecue or Sunday brunch.

"Nothing is going on," Kathryn said and laughed, albeit unconvincingly. "I just wondered if you could spare your old mother a summer afternoon."

"Mom . . . what's up?"

"Why must anything be up?" her mother queried. "But since you asked, there is the private reception Ethan's having to celebrate the opening of his new offices in Del Mar."

"I thought the party was planned for September."

"It is, honey. This is different, a more intimate gathering of a few close friends."

Sydney knew her mother clung to the hope that one day she and Ethan would look into each other's eyes, and admit they were hopelessly, madly in love. She had visions of being locked in Ethan's office with him, while their mothers—frequent co-conspirators and erstwhile Cupids—stood guard outside.

With that scenario in mind, she asked, "How intimate, exactly?"

"You should see how cleverly the architect remodeled the office," her mother said, ignoring the question. "The library is stunning. Floor-to-ceiling bookcases, of course, but the fourth wall is glass."

"Mom?"

"You should see the ocean view, and there's a huge fireplace to read by on those chilly nights when the fog rolls in—"

She tried again. "Mother?"

"What is it, dear?"

"I can't get away, period," she said, matter-of-factly. "This is a very complicated murder case, and work has to come first."

"Not even for one day?"

"Not even." She stood up and paced as far as the phone cord would permit. "No one expects Ethan to take a day off from court to fly in and see me—"

"But that's different—"

"Why is it different? He's an attorney, I'm a private investigator. This is my career, and I take my professional obligations seriously. So no, I won't kiss off my work on a whim . . . but I'm sorry if I ruined your plans."

"Plans? There isn't a plan!"

"Really, Mom?"

"Heavens, Sydney, you make it sound like I've concocted a sinister plot to manipulate your life!"

"The thought has occurred to me once or twice." She sat on the futon and tucked her bare legs beneath her. "Listen, if there's nothing else, I have to call Hannah before it gets too late."

"Well, I won't keep you. But remember, dear . . . you can always change your mind."

Hannah DeWilde answered on the first ring, as briskly efficient as ever. A violin played Mozart discreetly in the background, a marked contrast to the terminally peppy rock-and-roll that had serenaded Sydney at every turn since she'd arrived in Reno.

"Sydney," Hannah said, "I'm so glad you called. I'm on my way out to have a late dinner with a friend, but I wanted to let you know there'll be a package coming for you in the morning by Federal Express. You'll need to be there to sign for it."

"A package of what?"

"Materials related to the Foster case. It seems Xavier overlooked a journal that was given to him, which belonged to Laura Foster."

That piqued her interest. "Laura's journal? Did he say where he got it?"

"Actually, he made a distinct point of not saying, if you get my meaning."

"I do," Sydney sighed. Her partner dearly loved a little intrigue, and wasn't above manufacturing it if doing so served his needs. As long as he wasn't sticking her with purloined evidence, she didn't mind humoring him. "Anything else?"

"I believe he found more of his notes, along with assorted odds and ends related to the local news coverage of your case. He packed the box himself, so I can't be more specific than that."

"Okay, I'll keep an eye out for the FedEx truck."

"It shouldn't hold you up too awfully; they should be there by ten A.M."

"No problem." In the thirteen years she'd been an investigator, she hadn't run into many people who were eager to answer questions before ten o'clock anyway. "Anything else?"

"No, except that Trouble has been hanging around your door. I hope that's not an omen," Hannah said.

Trouble was the black and white guard-cat who belonged to the lady in 129 in Sydney's apartment complex. Hannah also lived in the building with Galaxie, a pure white feline charmer with one blue eye and one green.

Absurdly or not, Sydney felt a pang of homesickness. "I don't mind a little Trouble in my life. Give him a cookie for me, would you?"

"I will indeed. Now I really must be on my way or I'll be late."

"Thanks, Hannah. Wish Xavier good luck in court tomorrow, and tell him I'll call him—" she hesitated, not wanting to promise more than she could deliver "—in a day or two."

Sydney took a few minutes to gather her thoughts before she dialed Ethan's number. Listening to the line ring, she could almost visualize him, walking across the room to pick up the phone.

And then she heard his voice, as familiar to her as her own. She had known him all of her life, had grown up living just across the street, and yet there were moments like this when she felt they were strangers. That she didn't know him at all.

"Ethan," she said, "it's me."

"Sydney, hi."

The tone of his voice when he said her name made her

pulse quicken. "I'm sorry it's so late, but I just got in, and—"

"It doesn't matter. I'm glad you called; I wasn't sure you would."

"Why not?" she asked, and instantly regretted it. There were any number of reasons for her not to have called Ethan, starting and ending with Mitch. She added in a rush, "I hope you don't think I've been avoiding you."

Ethan laughed. "You mean, by leaving town?"

"Among other things, yes." The sad truth was, she *had* been avoiding him for some time now—and undoubtedly he knew why.

"None of that matters, Sydney. But we need to talk. Privately, in person. Soon."

"Is that a good idea, do you think, considering?"

"Considering what?"

"The circumstances, *our* circumstances. I'm getting married, Ethan."

He was silent for a moment. "Have you set a date?"

Ethan was too skilled as an attorney to break the cardinal rule of lawyers—never ask a question if you don't know what the answer will be—which meant that more than likely, he'd been talking to her mother, who was, no doubt, a veritable fountain of information about her plans. "Not yet, but—"

"But what?"

"We're going to. Ethan, nothing has changed. I'm not delaying the wedding because I'm uncertain or confused."

"Not even a little confused?"

She knew he was referring to the encounter they'd had back in April, the night he'd shown up unannounced at her door. His timing was sorely off—given that she was by then engaged to Mitch—and his delivery was uncharacteristically hesitant, but Ethan had finally told her that he was in love with her.

He had taken her into his arms—she had gone willingly enough—and kissed her with a hunger that left her trembling.

As often as she had dreamed about him growing up, and all of the years spent yearning for his touch hadn't prepared her for the reality of Ethan's insistent kisses. She had given in, for just that one impulsive moment, to the sensation of his mouth, the urgency of his hands, the heat of his body, and she had pressed herself full-length against him—

"Maybe I *was* confused," she said, closing her eyes, trying to block the memory of that night from her mind, "but only for the duration."

"The duration? You make it sound like we were at war. That's not at all how I remember it."

"I think I'm at war with myself." She got to her feet, suddenly restless, and carried the phone with her over to the front window. Looking out to the west, she saw the mountains silhouetted against the twilight sky, the highest peak still capped with snow. "But I can't fight that battle now. I'm sorry, but I just can't."

"Have you considered not fighting it at all?"

That made her smile. "I've never been one for surrender."

"And you know I meant what I said."

"Don't, please."

"I love you, Sydney. I *think* I always have, but I know I always will. I'm not giving up."

"Good night, Ethan," she said when she could trust her voice, and hung up quickly before he could respond. Only then did she realize that she was crying.

There was no answer at Mitch's house, so she dialed his

direct number at the police department. The line rang ten or more times before an unfamiliar voice answered and advised her that Lieutenant Travis was at the site of a gang shooting in Pacific Beach.

After hanging up, she sat for a moment, twisting her engagement ring around her finger. *Have you set a date?* The question haunted her, in part because she couldn't deny that she and Mitch had not even come close to setting a wedding date. But why hadn't they? The answer she offered when anyone asked was that they were both so very busy with their respective careers.

 . . . *a little confused?*

No, she thought, damn it, I'm not.

But her heart ached. Ethan was her first love. What had started as a schoolgirl crush when she was thirteen—and Ethan was twenty-one—had evolved over the years into an exceptional intimacy that stopped just short of romance. The difference in their ages complicated matters, as did Ethan's stubborn insistence on playing big brother, but she had been more or less content to let the relationship unfold in its own time . . .

That changed when she moved to Los Angeles for five years to train as an investigator with Dunn Security & Investigations, one of the premier detective agencies in the country. Working twelve-hour days, six and sometimes seven days a week, she only rarely made the drive down the coast to San Diego.

Midway through her training, Ethan had startled everyone by getting married. His marriage to Jennifer Miller lasted all of ten months before it self-destructed from what Ethan called "irreconcilable boredom."

At that point, Sydney had backed away. She still cared for him deeply, but there was an emotional distance between them that hadn't been there before.

And then Ethan had introduced her to Mitch.

It hadn't been a happily-ever-after situation with Mitch either—far from it—but like the tenacious cop he was, Mitch pursued her, and wouldn't take no for an answer.

Eventually, her answer changed.

Nevertheless, she did not want to hurt Ethan. There was so much history between them, a lifetime of memories, so many unresolved feelings . . . and that kiss.

"Knock it off," Sydney said aloud, "and get back to work."

The remedy to any upheaval in her personal life had always been her work, and she seized it. Consulting her notebook, she dialed the number for Erin Cross.

At midnight, the phone rang.

Sydney sat up in bed and turned on the light before answering. "Hello?"

"Did I wake you?" Mitch asked.

"Not really." Which was true; although physically tired, her mind was racing, and she hadn't been able to sleep. Just hearing his voice, though, eased her anxiety dramatically. "I'm glad you called; I tried to reach you at home earlier."

"It'll be awhile before I make it home. I'm pulling a twenty-four hour shift on a multiple homicide down by the beach."

In the background, Sydney could hear the faint roar of the waves breaking on the sand, intermingled with the customary static of radio traffic on the police band. "What happened?"

"By the look of it, a bunch of gang-bangers were trying to re-create the gunfight at the O.K. Corral, only with semi-automatics, which makes for a bloody mess. But forget that . . . I miss you."

Sydney smiled and reached over to turn out the lamp. Bathed in the soft glow of moonlight, she stretched lazily and said, "Why don't you tell me how much, Lieutenant? And in detail . . ."

Eleven

Friday

As a consequence of Xavier's indecipherable handwriting, the FedEx driver mistook a seven for a two and thus was late delivering her package in the morning, which set off a domino effect in that she was subsequently late leaving for her ten-thirty appointment with Erin Cross.

It also meant she didn't have an opportunity to review the materials the X-Man had sent her. And of course being late predetermined that every traffic light she came to would be red.

Such was life.

The Law Offices of McGill & Cross were located in a two-story red brick building that overlooked the Truckee River, near downtown Reno.

Parking was at a premium, but she maneuvered the Probe into a tight space between a plum-colored 1960 Ford Falcon Futura convertible and a turquoise-over-white Nash Rambler of indeterminate year.

The Rambler driver showed up as she was locking the car a minute later. He looked to be in his early forties, and color-coordinated with his car in white tennis shorts, a turquoise polo shirt and Nikes. "It'll never be a classic," he called to her cheerfully with a nod at the Probe, then got into the Rambler.

Backing out, he honked at her—or more accurately, beeped—and the car putted off like a wind-up toy, while one

102

of her mother's favorite songs, "Wayward Wind" by Gogi Grant, drifted from the open windows.

As she approached the main entrance to the building, a willowy brunette opened the door, a tennis racquet in one hand.

"Is he gone?" the brunette asked.

"Excuse me?"

"Mr. McGill," she said distractedly, and described the man who'd just driven off. "He forgot his racquet again, but I guess it doesn't matter, since his tennis date called to cancel . . ."

As under-powered as the Rambler seemed to be—whether it qualified as a classic or not—Sydney was tempted to suggest that the brunette run after it, but she resisted the urge. "Sorry, he left."

"Damn," the brunette breathed. "Guess who's going to be in a bad mood when he gets back. As if *she* isn't short-tempered enough."

"At least it's Friday," Sydney consoled.

The *she* in question was none other than Erin Cross.

Ms. Cross's office was almost militantly feminine. Decorated in pastel shades of pink, cream, and pale green, it featured French provincial furnishings amid an astonishing array of ruffles and frills. There was, curiously, a six-foot-tall brass unicorn in a corner of the room. Odd as that seemed, the unicorn did not look out of place.

In light of the fact that this was a law office, there were minor concessions to functionality—an IBM computer with modem and an upright laser printer—but style clearly outweighed form. The phone on the desk, perhaps tellingly, was a cream-colored, rotary-dial Princess.

In contrast to her surroundings, Erin Cross was dressed

conservatively in a tailored navy Versace suit and white silk blouse, with matching spectator pumps. She wore a slim gold watch on her left wrist, and fashionable gold hoop earrings, but no wedding ring.

Her blonde-streaked hair framed a sharply featured face that was more striking than pretty. Dark red lipstick drew attention to her slightly full lower lip.

"What can I tell you?" Erin Cross said, closing the office door and coming to sit behind the desk. "It's been so long, I'm afraid I won't be much help."

"Anything you can remember will help."

"Really," she murmured. Leaning back in her chair, she laced her fingers together over a shapely knee. "I gather by the fact he's hired you that Douglas has yet to come to terms with Sean's death."

"Murder often affects people that way."

"Murder?" Ms. Cross smiled condescendingly. "I was under the impression it was a suicide."

"That's the police theory," Sydney said. "It hasn't been proven. As for Douglas Foster, I don't know him very well, obviously, but I think he's determined to find an answer—"

"If there is an answer, after all this time." Her gaze was calculating. "I've had occasion to work with private investigators on many of my cases, and you'll forgive me for being blunt, but I haven't been impressed."

Sydney could say the same about lawyers, but she settled for a noncommittal smile.

"Are you that good?" Erin Cross persisted.

"Sometimes I get lucky."

"And modest, too, I see. You should get along fine with Douglas; he prefers women who are willing to keep a low profile."

Sydney got the distinct impression that she was being

baited and decided to cast a line of her own. "Do you mean Laura?"

Evidently that struck a nerve, because irritation flared in Erin Cross's blue eyes. "Laura Clifford was anything but modest."

"Did you know her well?"

"I didn't know her at all, but I knew the type. Pardon me if I seem callous, but Laura was a gold-digger from the word go."

Tell me how you really feel, Sydney thought wryly. "I was told that you had broken up with Sean before he and Laura met."

"Yes."

Single-word answers often indicated an area of sensitivity. On the other hand, the woman was an attorney, and as an attorney she knew better than to run off at the mouth. "How long before?"

"I don't know, years."

Sydney did not believe for a moment that Erin Cross could not recall more precisely when she and Sean had stopped seeing each other, but she let it pass . . . for now. "But you and Sean remained on good terms?"

"Yes. We didn't run into each other very often, but whenever we did, it was cordial. We even went out a couple of times."

"As an attempted reconciliation?"

"As old friends."

She wondered whose choice that had been. "Had you met Laura before the wedding?"

"Not to talk to, but—" her eyes narrowed slightly "—I did see her perform once, at Harrah's."

That was interesting. "How did that come about? I mean, was it accidental or did you go specifically to see her?"

"Actually, I did. I must admit I was curious as to what all the fuss was about."

"Fuss?"

"For want of a better term, yes. I'd heard that Sean was making a fool of himself over a showgirl here in town, and I thought I'd find out why."

"Was she any good?"

"Good at what?" Erin Cross asked, her tone plainly dismissive. "Taking off her clothes? I imagine she had a lot of experience at that."

"I was thinking more of dancing or—"

"If you can call it that. But no, I wasn't dazzled by her talent."

"Did she sing?"

"It wasn't a night at the opera, Ms. Bryant. No one pays to hear showgirls sing."

The only photos Sydney had seen of Laura thus far were over-exposed, black-and-white crime scene shots, but she took it on faith that Xavier had not exaggerated the young woman's appeal. "I've been told she was beautiful."

"Hmm."

She took that as a dissenting opinion. "Am I correct in assuming that the next time you saw her, it was at the wedding?"

"Yes."

"Did you talk to her?"

Erin Cross hesitated, then said, "I wished them both a long and happy life."

Which had not come to pass. "I spoke with Gary West yesterday, and he told me you were annoyed with him for taking you to the wedding—"

"Not for taking me," Ms. Cross interrupted, "but for using me to ambush the bride. I was furious at him when I found out that I was an uninvited guest."

"It must have been awkward."

"Awkward and humiliating. I can't begin to describe the look on Douglas Foster's face when he saw me. He must have thought it was all my doing, that I was trying to ruin the wedding."

"Why would he think that?"

"Why wouldn't he? The groom's former girlfriend shows up unannounced at the wedding . . . if that isn't a blueprint for disaster, I don't know what is."

"Even so," Sydney pointed out, "you stayed almost to the end."

"That's true, I did," Erin admitted, lifting her chin in defiance. "I didn't enjoy feeling like an interloper and I had a splitting headache, but I wasn't going to give anyone the satisfaction of running me off."

"Anyone meaning Laura Foster?"

"Anyone," she said icily, "meaning anyone."

"Did you have an opportunity to talk to Sean that day?"

"Yes, for a minute or two. I'd gone into the study to call a cab and afterwards I ran into him in the hall."

"Were you alone?"

Ms. Cross nodded. "For all of five minutes, yes. I apologized for being so naive, for unknowingly being drawn into another of Gary's pranks—"

"Gary said Sean took it in stride."

"Sean wasn't the least upset. Not about seeing me, anyway."

Sydney detected a hint of gratification in the woman's voice. "What did he say to you?"

"That there was no harm done. He reassured me that Laura didn't mind my being there and . . . he told me he was as happy as he'd ever been in his life. He said he was head over heels in love, that for the first time in his life, he understood what it meant to love someone unconditionally. He swore he'd walk through fire for her."

"How did that make you feel?"

Eyebrows raised, her tone incredulous, Erin Cross asked, "Are you implying that I was jealous?"

"Were you?"

"Not a chance."

"I've been told that you dated all through high school, which would suggest that your relationship was more serious than most."

"It was serious, but we were kids then. And it had been over for a long time."

"Even so, I imagine it must have hurt at least a little to hear someone you'd cared for say that he'd never loved you."

"That isn't what he meant."

"Isn't it?"

"Absolutely not. He wasn't rubbing my nose in it; he just wanted me to know how happy he was . . . and for me to be happy for him."

"Were you happy for him?"

"Believe it or not, I was." A tiny furrow appeared over the bridge of her nose. "Sean desperately needed to be loved. He pretended to be self-assured, but deep down inside—when it came to relationships—he was almost pathologically insecure."

Sydney regarded her with interest. "This is the first I've heard of it."

"Not everyone knew him as well as I did. Gary likes to brag that he and Sean were best friends, but Sean told me things that no one else knew."

"Such as?" she asked, not meaning it as a challenge, but willing to let Ms. Cross interpret it that way.

A flicker of annoyance showed in her eyes, and she frowned.

"He told me Alan tried to kill him when they were kids."

"What? How?"

"Alan tried to drown him in their uncle's pool. After Douglas was released from the hospital, the two of them moved in with him, as I'm sure you know. Boys being boys, they spent most of every summer in the pool."

"Surely they were supervised?"

"Not as closely as they should have been. Sean said they had a live-in nanny, but she was an older woman who tended to fall asleep on the job. Maybe she had narcolepsy, I don't know."

"No one noticed?"

"No one except the boys, and they weren't going to tell. Douglas had begun rehabilitation, and he was still dependent on others; he had around-the-clock nurses and a live-in physical therapist. I would guess that even though there were all these caregivers in the house, the boys weren't on the receiving end of much of it."

"So it would seem."

"Anyway, one day they were playing in the pool and got into an argument. Nobody was watching, so Alan pulled Sean under and held him there. Sean struggled free, but not before he nearly drowned. Sean said he only got away because he kicked Alan in the chin."

"What were they fighting about?"

Erin Cross shrugged. "Sean claimed he didn't remember."

"Did you believe him?"

"Of course I did; I was sixteen. I believed a lot of things then."

"How well do you know Alan?"

"Well enough to know I don't like him."

"Why is that?"

"I'll have to take the Fifth on that," she demurred. "I

gather you haven't met Alan yet?"

"No."

"Well, you're in for a treat."

One of many, Sydney thought, with a glance at her watch. She hadn't been able to reach Brad Goldwyn last night or this morning, but figured she might take a chance by driving up to Lake Tahoe and knocking on his door. And it was almost noon now, so she needed to get on the road. "Just a few more questions. What did you do after you left the reception at four-thirty?"

"I went home, took half a pain pill for my headache, and went to bed."

"That early in the day?"

"It didn't *feel* early."

"Were you able to sleep?"

"Like a baby," Erin Cross said, the suggestion of a smile on her face.

"Did you see anyone that evening? Talk to anyone on the phone?"

"Do I have an alibi, do you mean?"

"Something like that."

"No, I don't." There was an edge to her voice.

"What make of car were you driving in 1985?"

"In 1985? Let me think . . . I'd graduated from law school that May . . . I believe I was driving a Volkswagen Rabbit. It got great gas mileage, I remember that, because I went to school over the hill in Sacramento, and drove back to Reno almost every weekend."

"Why was that?"

"Why come home to Reno, you mean?"

"Yes."

Ms. Cross laughed. "Have you ever *been* to Sacramento? If so, you wouldn't ask."

"What I meant was, were you dating someone in town, or did you have family obligations—"

"Nothing like that. I was too busy to have much of a social life, and my parents were living in Las Vegas by then. But I'm a small town girl at heart, Ms. Bryant. Big cities wear me down. And I miss the cool desert nights."

"Okay. Last question: do you have any idea who might have killed Sean and Laura?"

"I haven't given it much thought, but if you're right and Sean didn't do it," Erin Cross said pensively, "then I'd have to say no, I don't."

Twelve

Rather than risk starvation on the way to Lake Tahoe, Sydney made a pit stop at an A&W Drive-In on Kietzke Lane. The place was swarming with cruisers, the lot filled bumper to shining bumper with classic cars.

Luck was with her, and she found a shaded spot between a tricked-out, chrome-laden 1950 Mercury convertible and a 1952 strawberries-and-cream Studebaker with delicate blue flames licking its sides. The portly Studebaker driver was wiping its fenders lovingly with what appeared to be a cloth diaper.

As always, the music was early rock'n'roll, Eddie Cochran's "Summertime Blues."

A carhop in shorts and a striped shirt took her order for a deluxe burger, curly fries, and—she couldn't resist—a root beer float. Waiting for her order, she made notes pertaining to the interview with Erin Cross, including a few questions that had been raised.

First and foremost, Sydney wondered whether a headache was the real reason Sean's ex-girlfriend had left the wedding reception early. As an excuse, it wasn't entirely implausible, but it certainly would have given Ms. Cross an opportunity to change clothes, get her own car, and follow the newlyweds if she were so inclined.

Could a woman have committed the murders? Very probably, although for some reason it didn't have that feel to Sydney. Nevertheless, everyone was a suspect at this stage of the investigation, and the "woman scorned" had both motive and opportunity, at least in theory.

There was also the matter of Sean's relationship with his brother. She hadn't made talking to Alan Foster a priority—assuming that he shared his uncle's concern for solving the case—but given his feelings for Laura and the childhood attempt to drown Sean, she decided to move his name up the list.

The waters were getting muddied . . . but then, that was normal in a murder case. As were the assorted perspectives of the victims by friend and foe; fitting together the bits and pieces of anyone's life based on rumors was tantamount to constructing a mosaic out of smoke.

Far too often the result was abstract and bore little resemblance to reality.

Her lunch arrived on a tray that mounted on the car window. The food was hot and fresh, the hamburger on the sloppy side, the way a good burger should be, and she made short work of it. The root beer float was in mortal danger from the August heat—she'd driven by a bank temperature gauge earlier that read ninety-six degrees—so she drank it quickly, risking brain-freeze.

Five minutes later, she merged onto the 395 Freeway, heading south.

According to the radio, there was a tie-up on the Mount Rose Highway, so she drove through Washoe Valley, past Carson City and took US 50 to Lake Tahoe. About halfway up the curving mountain highway, the sharp smell of pine filled the air. It was noticeably cooler, particularly along the shaded stretches of the road. Traffic was relatively light heading west, and she slowed her speed, the better to enjoy the spectacular views.

Coming around a bend, she caught sight of the lake, surrounded by dense forest and granite outcroppings, its waters a deep, clear blue. There were white cumulus clouds dotting the sky, playing peek-a-boo with the sun.

And there were still traces of snow at the higher elevations, lingering into summer, the source of the icy water of the lake.

What must it be like, Sydney wondered, to live amid such breathtaking beauty? Waking every morning to the whispering of the wind through the upper branches of hundred foot—and taller—Lodgepole and Ponderosa pines must be a curative for the soul, a natural antidote for stress.

There were signs of drought in the forest, dying trees scattered among the living, yellow and even red among the healthier green. And she'd passed a barren section of the mountain that still bore the traces of past fires, evidenced by the charred trunks of limbless trees, and scorched black earth.

But even there, there were signs of new life, tender young saplings reaching for the sky. It was nature's way to come forth from the ashes . . .

"And ours," she said softly.

A few miles further on, the traffic slowed and became congested. There were small businesses along the roadside, including an outboard motor repair shop, quaint antique boutiques, and even a supply store for prospectors. There were houses as well, obscured among the trees, accessible by steep, private driveways.

Shortly thereafter, the casinos came into view. In contrast to their brethren in Reno and Las Vegas, these were in keeping with their natural surroundings, with wood facades and subdued architecture. There were no pyramids here, no palaces from King Arthur's court, nor any neon monuments to excess.

The lakeside casinos were just as intent on separating a gambler from his or her money, but they were comparatively discreet about it.

On the street, tourists milled about, many carrying plastic buckets of coins as they sought the Holy Grail of gamblers: a slot machine ready to jackpot. There were a surprising number of children among the faithful. She'd read that casinos were trying to be kid-friendly, offering video arcades and the like, but that seemed to her less a genuine interest in making the casino a "family vacation destination" than a jaded attempt to solicit and nurture a new generation of gamblers.

Get 'em while they're young made good marketing sense, she supposed, although it did little to elevate the level of popular culture. Then again, wasn't pop culture something of a contradiction in terms?

Sydney drove across the state line into California, leaving the casinos behind on the Nevada side. There were still plenty of tourist traps, in the form of shops selling Tahoe-themed merchandise. T-shirts were the big draw, judging by the variety and sheer numbers of shirts displayed in windows, but there were also postcards and pins and mugs and hand-painted plates, as well as knick-knacks of every description, souvenirs whose main purpose would seem to be the collection of dust.

There were also a gluttony of food stands, selling soft-serve ice cream and yogurt, hot dogs and burgers, fish and chips, pizza by the slice, cotton candy of every hue, and whatever else was feasible to consume while walking the main strip.

Beyond that began the motor courts and lodges, most of

which were rustic to a fault. These offered Reasonable Rates and TVs in Every Room, plus HBO. Most were U- or L-shaped, with parking in front of the rooms. The lots were littered with oversized pine cones and a blanket of browned pine needles.

Business must be good; there weren't many Vacancy signs to be found.

The address she had for Brad Goldwyn was on Highway 50, curiously enough. She considered pulling off and trying to find a pay phone to call for directions, but the only phone booth she spotted was on the left side of the road, and attempting to make a left turn against the heavy flow of traffic held little appeal.

Worse yet would be trying to get back on the road. Perhaps the oxygen-thin air at this elevation had deprived her fellow drivers of the capacity for simple courtesy, but she didn't see any cars slowing to politely wave cross-traffic through.

Even paradise had a downside.

Besides, Goldwyn might not be home to answer the phone at two-thirty on a sunny Friday afternoon. By showing up in person, she could always knock on a few doors and ask his neighbors where he might be.

If the neighbors didn't know where Goldwyn was, at least she could ask a question or two about the man himself. As she'd told Martha Barclay, every bit of information helped in one way or another.

And as any gambler could tell you, sometimes you hit the jackpot.

It turned out Goldwyn was staying at one of the motor lodges. The Sierra Inn was a knotty pine wonder, with twenty units and a kiddie-sized heated pool. The units rented by the day or week, according to the faded sign on the office door, with a checkout time of twelve noon.

On the wood porch that fronted the office, there was a Pepsi machine that was wheezing and rattling like it was on its last legs. There were deep gouge marks on the machine where someone had pried it open to steal the money. As a deterrent, an index card over the coin slot advised that the change box was emptied daily.

"That'll work," Sydney said under her breath as she opened the office door.

The manager looked to be in his seventies, with wisps of white hair combed across his pink scalp. He was dressed in a khaki work shirt and pants, and wore scuffed leather slippers lined in red plaid. His blue eyes had the watery look of a life-long alcoholic, and he periodically rubbed at his eyes and bulbous nose with a stained—and visibly moist—handkerchief.

"Help you?" he asked in a sandpaper voice.

"Is Brad Goldwyn a guest here?"

The old man snorted. "A guest? Not by my reckoning, if you figure that guests eventually leave. He's a tenant, year-round."

Sydney displayed her investigator's license. "I'd like to talk to Mr. Goldwyn, if he's in."

The manager squinted at the license, then peered at her with barely disguised amusement. "He in trouble of some kind?"

"Not that I'm aware of."

"Huh." He sniffled into his kerchief. "Well, I hate to disappoint you, but he's been working a job all this week and I don't expect he'll be back until after dark. You can wait, if you want—"

"Do you know where he's working?"

The manager scratched his head. "I guess I do, since I'm

the one who recommended him for the job. He's sprucing up some cabins down by the lake for the new owner, who's a poker buddy of mine."

"I hate to bother him at work," Sydney said, "but it is important that I talk to him."

"Can't see the harm in it myself, but then I ain't the one paying his wages. Still—" he grinned "—the state labor laws say a man's entitled to take a break."

"Could you give me directions?"

"Better than that, I'll draw you a map," he said, reaching for a registration card. On the back, he sketched a virtual maze of roads, which he identified in his shaky script. When he finished he looked it over, then nodded in satisfaction as he handed it to her. "This'll get you there, if you keep your turns straight."

"I appreciate it." The card too was damp, and she slipped it into the outside pocket of her shoulder bag. At the screen door, she hesitated and glanced over her shoulder at the manager, who was watching her with the sly helpfulness of an older Norman Bates. "In case I miss him, what room is he in?"

"He's in 18, across the way there, by the laundry where the maid is."

Sydney looked where he was pointing and saw a blue-jeaned maid loading towels and linens onto a housekeeping cart. "Got it, thanks."

"Sure thing," he said, wiping his nose. The phone rang and he stepped over to an ancient PBX board to pick up a black handset. "Have a good one, you hear?"

Outside, she fed change into the soft drink machine and pushed the button for a Pepsi. As noisy and battered as the machine was, the can that clunked into the vending tray a moment later was icy cold to the touch, which restored her faith in refrigeration.

The Pepsi sustained her while she waited for a break in traffic to cross into the northbound lane; it took ten minutes before the driver of a Ryder truck slowed and allowed her to cut in front of him.

Half an hour later, she pulled to a stop in a dirt turnout on a dead-end road. There were six cabins, three on either side of the turnout, shaded by a grove of quaking aspen, leaves shimmering in the afternoon breeze. Dappled sunlight reflecting off her windshield made it hard to see at first . . .

Then she spotted three men lounging under one of the trees, near a green Coleman cooler. At this distance, she couldn't tell much more than that they were looking in her direction.

Back in April, she'd had a singularly unpleasant encounter with a young man who thought he was God's gift to women, after he'd lured her to a secluded site in the Anza-Borrego desert. Ever since then she'd played it safe, preferring to err on the side of caution if the circumstances warranted it.

This place was isolated enough to justify being circumspect. And three males were exponentially more dangerous than one.

The good news was that she had a valid concealed weapon permit from San Diego. As a rule, most California counties honored each other's permits. She reached under the car seat to retrieve the .38 that Wagner had loaned her, then slipped it in her jeans at the small of her back.

She got out of the car, but deliberately left the door slightly ajar and kept the keys in her hand.

"Hey," one of the men called, getting to his feet. "Are you lost?"

"I'm looking for Brad Goldwyn," Sydney said. As she got

closer she saw that one of them was a young man in his mid-teens, with the characteristic features—a sloping forehead, flattened nose, and round face—of Down Syndrome. He smiled shyly at her and ducked his head.

"Huey," the first man said, his expression grim, "go on inside and clean up, son."

Huey obediently stood up and hurried off into the closest cabin without a backward glance.

"You want me to stay, Brad?" the third man asked.

"I can handle this," Brad Goldwyn said. "I've been doing it for sixteen years."

Thirteen

"Doing what for sixteen years?" Sydney asked when they were alone.

Goldwyn made a face, of the as-if-you-didn't-know variety. "Doing a do-si-do with you people," he said, pointing an accusatory finger at her. "Only I'd like to sit this dance out, lady."

"You people? Who do you think I am?"

"Shit, I've been asking who the hell do you think you are all along—"

"Listen, I think you've mistaken me for someone else." She pulled out the bi-fold with her ID and showed it to him. "My name is Sydney Bryant, and I'm a private investigator. I've been hired by Douglas Foster—"

Goldwyn blinked as though startled. He took a step towards her and peered at her license. "Foster? Is this legit? You're not from Social Services?"

"It is and I'm not. I'm investigating the murders of Sean and Laura Foster."

"Well, I'll be damned."

"I'd like to talk to you," she added, "if you can spare a few minutes."

"Well," Goldwyn said, and grinned sheepishly. "I guess that's the least I can do after jumping sideways down your throat. Only can we keep it private? I don't want Huey to hear."

121

"Whatever you prefer." Sydney followed him to an open-ended carport between two of the cabins, where a gray-primered Land Rover was parked.

"Door's unlocked," he said, getting in on the driver's side.

"What year is this?" she asked, looking at him through the open window. "The Rover, I mean."

"It's a seventy-seven, why?"

"Just wondering. Are you the original owner?"

"Nah. I bought it cheap after the original owner flipped it on the Pyramid Highway. Lucky devil only broke an arm, but his wife went ballistic, and sold it out from under him to yours truly."

"What year was that?"

"Oh," he scratched his head, "in seventy-nine, I guess. Cost me two thousand dollars, and I had to do some body work, plus the frame was bent, but the wreck's still running, knock wood."

"Sounds like you got a deal." The passenger door screeched when she pulled it. The seat had been mended with silver duct tape many times—the frayed edges of a dozen layers of tape were visible—but she slid in and turned to face Goldwyn.

He looked to be in his late forties, his dark hair shot through with gray. The sun and time had lined his face, and there were furrows on his forehead and bracketing his mouth. His eyes were deep-set, the irises green with flecks of rust-brown.

The expression in his eyes, Sydney thought, was that of a man who had exorcized most of his demons, and seemed to be at peace with how his life had turned out. "Is Huey your son?" she asked.

"Huey is my heart," Goldwyn said. "And he's one super kid."

"He's what? Sixteen?"

"Seventeen and change. Look, I really don't mean to be rude, Miss Bryant, although I guess the horse has left the barn on that, but what does my boy have to do with Laura Clifford?"

"Foster," Sydney corrected. The wind had picked up and through the swaying trees, she caught a glimpse of the lake in the distance, its water a deep, icy blue. "I'm sorry, I don't mean to intrude, but I couldn't help but wonder . . . what you said about Social Services."

"Let's just say, the State isn't convinced that living with me in a hotel room with a hot plate is the best thing for Huey. And I'm not convinced that it's any of their damned business."

It clearly wasn't any of her business either, but she had to ask, "What about his mother?"

"Annie died of ovarian cancer when he was three. Now, can we change the subject?"

"Of course, I'm sorry. About Laura Foster . . . you were a guest of hers at the wedding?"

"True enough."

"Did you know her well?"

Goldwyn smiled, tugging on his right ear. "I thought I did, until she told me she aimed to marry a rich guy. After that, I wasn't sure."

"How did you meet?"

"I was living in Reno, taking care of Huey while his mama was in the hospital over in Palo Alto, and about all I could afford for recreation was the park at Virginia Lake. Huey was, what? A year and a half, I guess. Anyway, he loved to go see the ducks. Something about those ducks made him laugh— heaven only knows what—but when that boy got to laughing, it was contagious."

Sydney smiled.

"Laura was living in an apartment a few blocks away from the park, so she came almost every day. She and Huey took to

each other . . . she told me they were kindred spirits."
Goldwyn sighed. "She said he had an ancient soul."

"And you became friends?"

"Very good friends. Back in those days, I couldn't scramble
an egg without having to call the fire department, so she'd
come over to fix dinner for us. Not that Laura was a whiz in the
kitchen, but she could warm up a can of Spaghetti-O's and
make it seem special."

"That's impressive." Sydney laughed.

"It impressed the hell out of me. And she didn't seem to
mind if she got Spaghetti-O's in her hair. Huey hadn't quite
gotten the hang of how a spoon worked. But we had a good
time, the three of us."

"How did Annie feel about that?"

Goldwyn frowned. "Annie didn't know, but even if she
had, we were already divorced."

"Did you and Laura go out together?"

"Like a date, you mean?"

Sydney nodded. "You were single, and Laura was an attractive young woman . . ."

"Oh yeah," he said softly. "She could turn a man's head,
easy. But we never had that kind of a relationship; we were
friends."

That seemed at odds with the scene that Martha Barclay
had described, but she let it pass for the time being. "Was
Laura dating Sean?"

"Not when we met, she wasn't."

"Someone else?"

He hesitated, grimaced, then said, "Let me put it this way:
a girl with her looks is bound to attract a lot of men. Particularly with the job she had."

"As a showgirl, did she ever have a problem with men ha-
rassing her at work?" Stalking had come to the forefront in

1989 with the murder of actress Rebecca Schaeffer, but it had been going on much longer that.

"If she did, she never mentioned it to me."

"Did you ever see her perform?"

"Not a chance."

Sydney regarded him curiously, hearing a hint of anger in his response. "Any reason in particular?"

"I didn't think it was a good idea. If you were hungry and broke, would you torture yourself by thinking about food all day?"

"My guess is that food would be all I could think about, whether I wanted to or not."

Goldwyn squinted at her. "Well, there's that. All right, I'll admit, I would have liked to been more than a friend to Laura, but she never showed an interest in me, not in that way."

"Is that why you kissed her on her wedding day?"

"Heard about that, did you?"

"In my line of work, I hear a lot of things. But I try not to jump to conclusions."

"Glad to hear it. The sorry truth is, I'd had too much to drink, and—" his smile looked pained "—she was so damned radiant, it hurt to look at her."

"Were you in love with her?"

"Not in love, no. But I loved her in my own way, for what she'd done for Huey, and how nice she'd been to me. You know, it isn't often that a woman like that would give a guy like me the time of day."

"That sounds a little bitter," she noted.

"Maybe it is. Laura was out of my league, and I knew it from the start." He shrugged, then held his hands out to her. His palms were callused, his knuckles were scraped, and his left thumbnail was black and purple. "I've been a handyman all of my life, and the Lord knows, I haven't made much of myself. If it weren't for Huey keeping me on the straight and narrow, I'd be even less than this."

"I don't know . . . raising Huey on your own is quite an accomplishment."

"Huey got the worst of that bargain," Goldwyn said. "The point is, I had a little crush on Laura, although if I hadn't been drinking, I'd never have kissed her. But she didn't seem to be upset about it."

Recalling what Martha had told her, Sydney asked, "Not even when you suggested that she'd married a boy?"

"Shit! Did I say that?"

"Evidently."

He groaned. "Well, I didn't mean it. I didn't even know the guy."

"You hadn't met before that day?"

"Not to talk to. I saw him a couple of times when Laura would have him stop by my place to pick her up after she'd spent an afternoon with Huey."

Which sounded rather cozy, Sydney thought. "What was your impression of Sean, other than that he was—what did you call him—a rich guy?"

"My impression was that Sean Foster was one very lucky son of a bitch."

"And yet," she said carefully, "he wound up dead."

"So did Laura." Goldwyn met her eyes, then looked away, absently running two fingers along the arch of the steering wheel. After a moment, he added, "I had nothing to do with that."

"I wasn't accusing you—"

"Weren't you? Hell, I make a very convenient suspect, if I do say so myself."

"How is that?"

"I'm the outsider, or haven't you noticed?"

"Actually," Sydney said, "I hadn't."

"Then you haven't been paying attention. Who else would make such a great fall guy? Mr. Foster is above suspicion, and as for Alan, not in a million years would the police go after him. And their cousin, Randy? Not likely, since he's related by blood—"

"Are you suggesting that one of them did it?"

"I'm not suggesting anything. Except that I've been waiting to be accused for fifteen years."

"Why is that?"

"Because all along I've felt like I had a bull's eye on my back."

"Sorry, you've lost me. My information is that the police have consistently maintained that Sean murdered Laura. Even now that his remains have been identified, they're claiming he committed suicide—"

"The cops love mind games," he interrupted, his hands gripping the wheel. "They lie through their teeth when it suits them."

This wasn't the first time Sydney had heard that opinion voiced. Anti-authority sentiment was reaching a high water mark in the country, and conspiracy theorists were coming out of the woodwork.

"Think about it," Goldwyn persisted, his manner calm. "There were nine people at the wedding, and two are dead. Of the seven remaining, you have to eliminate the old man because he's in a wheelchair. Cross off the brother and the cousin, and that leaves four."

"Go on."

"So who's left? The best man, that guy Gary? Shit, he dresses too well—"

Startled, Sydney couldn't help but laugh. "That doesn't make him innocent."

"Yeah, but money talks," Goldwyn said with a weary smile. "It always has, and always will."

"What makes you think Gary West has money?"

"For starters, he bent my ear for half an hour about how he was making it rich. He and Sean had some kind of a deal going, he said. The two of them would be rolling in dough come Christmas, and he'd be driving a Porsche by New Year's Eve."

"But that fell apart when Sean disappeared," Sydney pointed out.

Goldwyn shrugged. "Easy come, easy go."

Only it never feels that way, she thought.

"And then—" he went on "—there's the girlfriend, what was her name?"

"Erin Cross."

"That's the one. I heard Mr. Foster congratulate her for graduating from law school. Somehow, I can't see the police giving her grief."

"You never know."

"Sometimes you do. If the police could have hung this on me back then, they would have."

"Did they try?"

"They thought about it, long and hard, if only to spare Douglas Foster the embarrassment of having Sean named a suspect. But—" he grinned "—I had an alibi. Hell, I had the *only* alibi."

She'd read the brief statement Brad Goldwyn had given in 1985; nowhere was there any mention of an alibi. "This is the first I've heard of it."

"That doesn't surprise me. But I do. After I left the reception, I went straight home because Huey was coming down with a cold. He had a fever when I got there, and the sitter said he had thrown up a couple of times. So I took him to the emergency room."

"Which of course would have a record."

"Damned straight. It was a Saturday, and the place was packed. I signed in at 5:42, and we didn't get out of there until a little after eight."

"You remember the exact time?"

"I more than remember it. I'd have had them tattoo it on my body if I thought that would hold up in court." He reached around and pulled out a thin leather wallet. "And I kept my copy of the consent form."

Sydney watched him thumb through the wallet's contents and pull out a folded pink sheet.

Goldwyn smiled as he spread the paper out on the seat between them. "It's a little faded, but you can still read it."

The information typed on the sheet included Huey's full name, address and birth date. The complaint read: Fever x 2 hours, congestion, vomiting x ?, and lethargy. She knew full well that a minor child could not be left unattended in an emergency room without that fact coming to someone's notice.

Brad Goldwyn was identified as the Responsible Party, his occupation given as carpenter. He had signed the Consent to Treatment form, and printed the word "Father" on the line below, specifying his relationship to the patient.

Alma White, RN, had witnessed his signature with her own, and added the date of August 3, 1985, and the time of 5:42, with P.M. circled beside that.

In the upper right hand corner was a block for Time of Discharge. In it, someone had written 8:07, and drawn a line through P.M.

"If you had this," Sydney said thoughtfully, "why would the police suspect you?"

"Damned if I know. But they wanted me. If they could have made my alibi go up in smoke, they would have." He began to refold the consent form, almost reverently. "Whoever they claim their suspect was, my gut tells me that this piece of paper is all that stood between me and a murder charge."

"And yet," she frowned, trying to make the pieces fit, "you were the police source for the charge that Sean and Laura had been arguing on their wedding day."

"I'd forgotten about that. Still, you have to understand, even with an alibi, I was desperate for the cops to leave me alone. I would have told them just about anything to get them off my back."

"Wasn't it true?"

"It was true, but I might have exaggerated it—" he held his thumb and index finger a quarter inch apart "—maybe just a little."

"Do you want to tell me about it?"

"There's not much to tell," Goldwyn said. "I was wandering around the house, trying to imagine what it must be like to live there. Anyway, to make a stupid story short, I made a wrong turn somewhere along the line and ended up in, I think, Sean's room."

"Go on."

"I should have hightailed it out of there, but I needed to use the, uh, facilities. I was in the private bath when I heard voices in the other room. I recognized Laura's voice and peeked through the crack in the door. She and Sean were arguing, but not loudly. You know the way people whisper, kind of urgently?"

Sydney nodded. "What were they saying?"

"I only heard bits and pieces. I did hear Sean say 'Can't it wait?' a couple of times. He sounded angry, but his back was to me, so I couldn't see his face. Laura looked really upset, and she kept repeating, 'If you don't tell him, I will.' "

"Meaning what?"

"Damned if I know. He also said something like, 'Let me do this my way' and then she said, 'I don't think you want to do it at all.' "

Fragments of conversation taken out of context were the verbal equivalent of hieroglyphics; interpreting them took skill . . . and luck. "Anything else you remember?"

"Nope. That was pretty much that."

"Is that what you told the police?"

"More or less. Except I let the cops believe that Sean was yelling, and Laura was crying, which wasn't strictly the truth," Goldwyn said, as he tucked his alibi back into his wallet.

She noticed, then, a color photograph in a clouded plastic holder. It was of a young woman and a little boy, no older than two, wearing a white sailor suit. The boy was Huey, but . . .

"Who's that?"

Goldwyn frowned. "Don't you know?"

"That's Laura?"

Without a word, he withdrew the picture from its sleeve—where it wanted to stick—and handed it across to her.

Laura Clifford Foster was stunningly beautiful. Her skin was lightly tan, her complexion flawless. A winsome strawberry blonde, her hair an artful disarray of ringlets, she smiled flirtatiously at the camera, her blue eyes sparkling.

Her arm was around Huey, who was looking up at her as though in wonder . . .

"Huey misses her still," Brad Goldwyn said. "I sure hope you find out who killed her."

Sydney handed the photograph back, meeting his glance. "I'll do my best."

Fourteen

The last question she asked Brad Goldwyn before heading back to Reno was whether he knew how to reach Tiki Everly.

"Who?"

"Laura's other wedding guest."

"Oh, right, Tiki," he said, a faraway look in his eyes. "Funny, but I'd forgotten all about her. Tiki Everly . . . talk about a flake!"

"Did you know her well?"

"I didn't know her at all. I mean, I danced with her at the reception, but the lady was a little too weird for my taste. She was into astrology, UFOs, and all that bunk. I'm not sure where or how Laura met her, but it wasn't in the neighborhood."

"I take it you haven't seen her since?"

"Not hardly. Why? Haven't you been able to track her down?"

"Not so far."

"Huh. Well, maybe the mother ship finally came and took her home."

"That might explain it," Sydney said with a smile. "Then again, it could be she's awfully good at playing hide and seek."

"Ask the cops," he suggested. "They're good at dogging people."

Only as a last resort, she thought. With any luck it wouldn't come to that.

Driving away, she looked in the rearview mirror and saw Huey come out of a cabin and walk over to his father, who gave the boy a hug.

"Good luck," she said to their reflections. The fact was, she felt a measure of relief at being able to cross Goldwyn off her mental list of suspects. Her allegiance had to be—and truly was—with Sean and Laura, but she would have hated to sacrifice Huey's happiness in the process of solving the mystery.

There were more than enough victims of that August night already . . .

She arrived at the condo shortly after six P.M. to find a florist's van blocking the garage, and a delivery man at the front door. There were a couple of guest parking spaces, and she pulled the Probe into the closest one. As she walked across the drive, the delivery man came down the steps towards her, a square white box in one hand and a clipboard in the other.

"Are you Ms. Bryant, by chance?"

"Yes."

"Then this is for you." He handed her the box. "I need your signature on line ten."

Sydney accepted the clipboard and signed her name. "I wasn't expecting flowers," she said, returning the clipboard and pen to him.

"That's the best time to get 'em." He grinned at her. "Particularly since I've made three trips to deliver them. And pardon me for asking, but I gotta know . . . is your first name really Sydney?"

"It really is," she answered absently, pulling the gift card free of the tape affixing it to the box.

"You sure don't look like any Sydney I've ever met," he said. "Have a nice day, you hear?"

"I'll do what I can."

The small envelope had been sealed and she peeled the flap back as she walked up the front steps. At the door she stopped to extract the card. There was an embossed gold heart on the card, which read:

Dear Sydney;

> *Physicists tell us that entropy is the final proof that time only moves forward. Poets tell us that time waits for no man. I'd rather believe in the Stones, that time is on our side.*

Love,
Ethan

"Entropy?" Sydney unlocked the front door and went inside. "Somebody's obviously been working way too hard."

She took the box into the kitchen where she used a steak knife to slice through the decorative silver and blue tape securing the lid. Inside, nestled in tissue paper, was an orchid corsage.

It was lovely. There were actually three orchids, amid a twist of dark purple satin ribbon. There was but a whisper of fragrance to the flowers, as ethereal as time itself, she thought.

"What is he up to now?" she asked, gently touching a silken petal.

She had only a few seconds to puzzle over it before the phone rang. She returned the corsage to its box and put the box in the refrigerator, then walked over to answer the call before the machine picked up.

"Ms. Bryant?" a male voice inquired.

"Speaking."

"This is Alan Foster. My uncle informs me that you're investigating my brother's death."

Sydney noticed that he hadn't mentioned Laura, and wondered why. Perhaps he didn't trust himself to say her name? Or maybe, after fifteen years, he'd convinced himself that she didn't matter . . .

"Yes," she said, "I certainly am. As a matter of fact, I'd very much like to talk with you, at your convenience, of course—"

"Any time," he interrupted. "Anything I can do, just say the word."

Which was more or less what she would expect him to say. "How about tomorrow morning, nine o'clock?"

"Fine, that'll be fine."

That would give her an opportunity to review Laura's diary and whatever else was in Xavier's mystery package. "If you'll tell me how to get to—"

"There is one little problem, Ms. Bryant. You see, I have company this weekend . . . it would be, well, awkward to talk at the house. Would it be terribly inconvenient for me to come there?"

"Not at all," she assured him—it would be nice to have an interviewee come to her for a change—and gave him directions to the condo.

"Very good. I'll see you tomorrow, then, at nine A.M.," he said abruptly, and slammed the receiver down with enough force to register on the Richter scale.

"A simple good-bye would have been nice," Sydney said to the dial tone and hung up.

She took a knife with her into the front room to cut open the reinforced tape that sealed the parcel from Xavier. Her partner was clearly from the if-a-little-tape-is-good-a-lot-of-tape-is-better school of thought.

There had to be six or seven yards of tape crisscrossed over the top. Not knowing exactly what was inside the box meant she couldn't make use of the slash-and-burn technique she'd perfected as a child, opening her gifts on Christmas morning . . .

It took the better part of five minutes, but she finally sawed through the last filament of tape. Under the lid was a layer of bubble wrap, and beneath that she found a thin book, bound in coffee-colored leather, the word Journal stamped onto its cover in gold letters.

The name Laura Clifford was printed neatly on the front page, in black ink. A phone number—presumably her own—had been written in the lower right hand corner, with a notation to "Call if found."

The first dated entry was January 1, 1985. The last was July 30th, of that same year.

She intended to review the journal in its entirety as time permitted, but for now, she settled for reading the last entry.

Only two days until the wedding! I can hardly believe how quickly the time has flown. Two more nights as a single girl, and I'll be a married lady.

Finally! And forever!

Mrs. Sean Foster—I love the sound of that! I love him even more.

I had the final fitting for my wedding gown today.

Sean wasn't supposed to be there, but he showed up in a silly mood, wanting to elope.

I told him it was bad luck to see the bride in her gown before the wedding, and he said I shouldn't be so superstitious. I didn't tell him what Tiki said about the black dream.

Tomorrow is my last night at work.
Friday is my last night in this apartment.
Saturday is the first day of my new life.
I can't wait!

Sydney closed the journal thoughtfully. What on earth, she wondered, was the black dream?

Placing the book on the end table, she turned her attention to the box. There was a padded envelope inside which had been stapled shut. The label on the envelope was from Rainbow Video Transfer Service in El Cajon.

Another video? Of what?

She hadn't gotten around to reviewing the crime scene footage yet, primarily due to time constraints but also out of concern that the videotape was in poor condition because of its age. Plus she doubted that the TV news coverage from 1985 would be definitive enough to add anything substantial to what she already knew from the still photographs and police reports.

On the other hand, it was her practice to be as thorough and meticulous as possible. She hadn't completed as much of the groundwork on this case as she would have preferred at this stage of the investigation, and that troubled her in a fundamental way. Working in a strange city without having the resources of her office as backup accounted for part of the delay, but as far as she was concerned, virtually nothing justified being ill prepared.

Without adequate preparation, it was far too easy to miss something of importance. In a murder case, that simply was inexcusable.

Tonight was as good a time as any to catch up, she thought, starting with the tapes. But first, there were two more items in the box: a spiral notebook in which Xavier had evidently kept track of his off-duty investigation, and several blue-cased rolls of Super 8 film in a Ziploc bag. Also in the bag was a yellow cash receipt for $37.66 issued by Rainbow Video Transfer Service—dated yesterday—from which she gathered that the rolls of film were the source material for the new videotape.

The sixty-four thousand dollar question: who was the source of the film—and the diary—and how had they come to be in Xavier's possession?

Sydney turned on the television and inserted the new tape into the VCR. Theater owners might not agree, but she was glad that cocooning was "in" and that so many people rented movies to watch at home, since a VCR was the one piece of equipment she hadn't brought with her.

It was apparent from the over-exposed first frames that the Super 8 film hadn't been edited at all before being transferred to video, but the washed-out images and jiggling camera were only a momentary distraction from the subject of the footage—Laura.

Laura at eighteen, Sydney guessed, in the first reel. She was dressed in a gold leotard, with her gorgeous reddish-blonde hair reaching nearly to her waist. She wore white ankle boots with leather fringe and stacked heels, and was twirling a baton.

There was something coltish about her, as though she'd startle easily, and her long, slender legs seemed perhaps a little ungainly.

She was performing on a makeshift outdoor stage, with blue sky overhead. Twirling the baton, she danced to David Bowie's "Young Americans" which blasted from a boom box that sat on a card table to the rear of the stage. The sound quality was remarkably good, considering it was at best third generation.

Two minutes in, Laura tossed the baton, did a cartwheel,

and caught the baton without missing a beat. A few seconds later, she flung the baton skyward, spun once, and did the splits . . . but missed the baton.

Or rather it missed her; she had to cover her head with both arms to keep from getting hit.

Looking straight into the camera, Laura stuck out her tongue and began to laugh.

"Allll right," David Bowie sang approvingly in the background.

"Turn it off." Laura giggled, drawing her legs to her and resting her chin on her knees. "Let me catch my breath, and we'll go again."

Off-camera, a gruff male voice said, "I'm almost out of film, so you might as well vamp it up."

"I told you," Laura purred, stroking a tanned knee, "I'm not that kind of girl."

"That's a shame," the cameraman lamented, zooming to a close-up at the same time he apparently walked towards the stage. "And a phenomenal waste of talent."

Laura merely smiled. Closer still, the camera adored her face, showing the flush of exertion coloring her high cheekbones, and a fine sheen of perspiration on her forehead and upper lip.

Fifteen seconds later, there was a flash frame, followed by black.

Sydney waited. As an investigator-in-training at Dunn Security & Investigations, she had occasionally used a Super 8 camera—the precursor to the omnipresent minicam—for surveillance, and she vaguely recalled that each roll of film had a playtime of approximately three to four minutes.

There were five rolls of film. Ergo, she expected there to be a total of fifteen to twenty minutes of material, plus intermissions.

The next segment began, of what appeared to be a small town beauty pageant. Laura was wearing a white dotted Swiss dress with a flared skirt, and three-inch heels. Her hair had been gathered to one side, where it cascaded over her shoulder and back.

She was one of three young women on a bandstand draped with red, white and blue bunting. The other contestants were visibly nervous, but Laura seemed remarkably composed, her smile relaxed.

The red-faced master of ceremonies mopped his brow with a handkerchief, then accepted a folded card from the judges. He crossed to a microphone and thumped it, testing to see if it was on.

The sound it made was like distant thunder.

"Folks, folks, if I could have your attention please." He hitched his thumbs inside of his suspenders as he waited for the crowd to quiet. "It is my distinct pleasure and an honor to present to you, the new Miss Sparkle for the annual Fourth of July Celebration, in the year of our Lord, 1981 . . . Miss Laura Clifford!"

Laura pantomimed the customary beauty queen's surprise, a wide-eyed look of overwhelming joy balanced with a dollop of demure self-restraint. She raised her hands to cover her face for a millisecond before smiling radiantly and stepping forward to accept her crown and sash from the outgoing Miss Sparkle.

Then, in lieu of flowers, the emcee handed her a silver wand with a five-pointed star at the end, not unlike the one Sydney had gotten at Sleeping Beauty's Castle in Disneyland when she was eight.

The film ended with Laura and Miss Sparkle of 1980 exchanging a carefully orchestrated embrace, kissing the air near each other's cheek.

Again there was a blinding flash frame, followed by video snow and white noise.

"Hold that thought," Sydney said, hitting the freeze button. There was something about watching home movies that made her want to nibble. She went to the kitchen for a slice of chocolate chip cheesecake and a Pepsi.

Returning to the living room, she sat Indian-style on the futon and hit Play on the remote.

The third film had been shot in the early morning, judging by the quality of the light. Barefoot, dressed in cut-off jeans and a red tube top, her hair caught up in pigtails, Laura wandered through a child's playground. She came down the slide, went across a sand pit on the rings, and—inevitably—wound up on the swings.

The sound track to the third segment was distinctly inferior, fading in and out, but Sydney could hear the faint rattle and creak of the chains as Laura swung. Pumping with the skill that most little girls master—and never forget—Laura went faster and faster, higher and higher, seemingly without effort.

Whoever was behind the camera did an excellent job keeping her in frame, catching glimpses of the exhilarated expression on her face. Closing her eyes, her lips slightly parted, Laura soared through the air, extending her legs and pointing her toes, then tucking them gracefully beneath the swing on the backswing.

Watching, Sydney could almost imagine the feel of the wind in her hair—

The doorbell rang.

"Damn it." Annoyed at the interruption—more than likely it was a sales-type peddling his or her wares—she considered ignoring it, but there was a slim possibility that it might be related to the case.

And as obsessive as she could be about her work, she couldn't stand not knowing. Taking a bite of cheesecake, she walked to the door with plate in hand so it would look as though she'd been disturbed while having dinner, or at the least, dessert. That wouldn't deter a hard-core sales rep—nothing short of light artillery would—but it was worth a try.

In the entry, Sydney paused for a second to glance through the peephole, took a startled breath, and opened the door.

"Ethan," she said in disbelief, "what are you doing here?"

Fifteen

"And," Sydney added, giving him the once over, "in a tuxedo, no less." He looked incredibly elegant, very much in his element, as though he'd been bred and born to money, which she knew, having grown up living across the street from his family, was far from the truth.

Ethan smiled. "Can't you guess?"

"Hmm. The airline instituted a dress code for passengers flying first class?"

"Not the worst idea I've ever heard, considering, but no."

"Then I haven't a clue." She stood aside and held the door open for him. "Still, I assume you're going to tell me, so come on in."

"I thought you'd never ask."

Sydney followed Ethan into the living room, then walked past him to turn off the videotape, pausing for a moment when she saw that Laura was dressed quite provocatively in a black satin bikini-cut outfit, complete with an ostrich-feathered and bejeweled showgirl's headdress. Her eyes were artfully made up, accentuated by gold glitter on her cheekbones that extended upward into her hairline.

There was roughly a light-year's distance stylistically between Laura's showgirl persona and that of a baton-twirling majorette. Mildly troubled by the abrupt metamorphosis, Sydney hit the Off button, and the screen went black.

She sat on the futon and tucked her legs beneath her, frowning as she raked the fork tines along the top of the cheesecake. Ethan had remained standing and was watching her, she knew, but feeling stubborn, she waited for him to speak.

After a moment, he cleared his throat. "Did you get the corsage?"

"I did, thank you." She took an infinitesimal bite of cheesecake and looked up to meet his eyes. "And the physics lesson about entropy was . . . instructive. But I'm not sure what the point is."

"The point is, I'm here to take you to the prom."

"What?"

"The prom, Sydney. You know, a magical evening of dancing in a gym decorated with crepe-paper streamers and Japanese lanterns. And between dances, we can sip watered down punch."

"I'm familiar with the concept," she said archly, "but why the prom?"

"Don't tell me you've forgotten."

In truth, she hadn't. Back in April, when they'd had their heart-to-heart, she'd told him what it had been like for her growing up with a world-class crush on him. Their conversation had echoed over and over again in her mind in the months since then. So she certainly had not forgotten, not at all.

Sydney closed her eyes for a few seconds, unnerved by the surge of emotion that accompanied the memory. When she could trust her voice, she said quietly, "Nothing can change the past."

"Maybe not, but that doesn't mean I can't learn from my mistakes. And I would love to take you to the prom. I know I'm a little late, but better late—"

"—than never, yes, I've heard." Only sometimes it wasn't.

"One night, Sydney, that's all I ask." He favored her with a boyish grin. "Just one night."

"It isn't that simple—"

"Nothing ever is," he agreed, "but there's no logical reason it has to be complicated, either. And I promise I'll have you home by the stroke of midnight."

Searching his eyes, she felt torn. Whatever his contention otherwise, the fact remained that the relationship between them had *always* been complicated. There was so much shared history, a compilation of significant moments in each of their lives—both good and bad—which created a bond much deeper and stronger than that of mere friends. Every memory she had of growing up included Ethan.

Most of her dreams had as well . . . until Mitch walked into her life.

Ethan sat on his heels in front of her, took the plate from her and put it on the end table, then took both of her hands in his. "Come on."

"You don't think it's inappropriate for us to go out? I am engaged."

"No, I don't," he said, smiling mischievously. "Why, do you think Mitch will mind?"

"Wouldn't you?"

"Ah, but that's my point. I never objected when he went after you—"

"Went after me? That sounds a little predatory, don't you think?"

"Doesn't it, though? Regardless, I respected your right to see whomever you choose."

"But you and I weren't engaged."

"That's irrelevant. If anything, Mitch should trust you precisely because you are engaged."

"All right," she said, finally. After all these years, she ought to know better than to argue with a lawyer. "But I'm pretty sure the fifties prom was last night—"

"No problem, I've arranged everything."

"—and, silly me, I don't usually pack a formal when I'm working a murder case."

"Don't worry, I've got it covered."

"How is that possible? No wait—don't tell me. My mother."

"I couldn't have done it without her," Ethan confirmed, and his expression turned serious. "I've got everything you need . . ."

He wasn't referring to a prom gown, she knew. Rather than delve into his not-so-hidden meaning, she got quickly to her feet and stepped around him. "If we're going to do this, I'd better get ready."

After a quick shower, she found a Saks Fifth Avenue box on her bed, along with a shopping bag containing a pair of black, strappy sandals with inch and a half heels, and black thigh-high hose.

A little kinky of Mom, she thought.

Likewise, the gown that her mother had selected for her would have gotten her suspended if she'd worn it to the Junior Prom. A dark sapphire blue in color and made of that pseudo-metallic fabric that had supplanted lamé, the dress had a revealing neckline and was to all extents and purposes backless.

It fit like a shimmery second skin, and when she walked, the long, slightly flared skirt seemed to flow caressingly around her legs.

The look was sophisticated and beguiling.

Studying herself in the mirror, Sydney shook her head. "Mothers. What happened to the woman who nearly fainted the first time I tried on a miniskirt?"

She wasn't particularly adept at styling her hair, but she managed to gather it back in a reasonable facsimile of a French twist, although she was relatively certain that the French would disavow any affiliation with the style. The best she could hope for was to avoid provoking an international incident . . .

A touch of mascara, a little lipstick, and she was ready to face the night.

"Wow," Ethan said as she came down the stairs. "You look fantastic."

Sydney smiled to disguise her self-consciousness and changed the subject. "Where is it that you're taking me when I really should be—"

"Working?"

"Exactly."

"An evening off won't get you drummed out of Workaholics Anonymous," he laughed.

"No, but it'll ruin my perfect attendance record." She glanced at her décolletage with a frown. There was rather more of her showing than she was accustomed to, front and back. "Although who knows? Maybe I'll win the evening gown competition."

"You've got my vote."

"Thanks . . . I think." She brushed by him, heading for the kitchen to get the corsage. In spite of her initial reluctance to play dress-up, she enjoyed the sound and the feel of the skirt swirling around her legs and ankles as she walked.

Taking the corsage from its box a moment later, she turned to see Ethan in the kitchen doorway, watching her with an expression that might even make her mother wonder at his intentions.

"You want me to do that for you?" he asked, indicating the wicked-looking, three-inch straight pin that came with corsage.

"I suppose it might cut down on the bloodshed . . ."

"Reason enough, I'd say." Ethan crossed to where she was waiting and took the corsage and pin from her, then stood in front of her. His fingers brushed against her bare skin. "Hold still."

All that was missing, she thought as he pinned the corsage to the thin strap of her gown, was her father taking pictures of them. Jonathan Bryant had died a week after she had graduated from college, and she missed him terribly, even now.

Remembering her father's ongoing battle with the automatic flash attachment of his expensive German 35mm camera, Sydney smiled wistfully. He had never quite got the hang of it, or of anything even remotely mechanical, for that matter. The flash was blindingly bright, which explained why most of the photographs in the family album made them look like fugitives on an FBI Most Wanted poster.

"What's the smile for?" Ethan asked as he finished securing the corsage.

He had not stepped back and Sydney was uncomfortably aware of his nearness; she could smell the light clean scent of his cologne. She retreated as nonchalantly as she could. "Just . . . reminiscing."

"About what?"

"My dad. If he was here—" her voice caught and she had to take a breath to steady it "—we'd be smiling at the camera until our faces went numb."

Ethan laughed. "That's right, I remember. Him and his super-nova flash."

"Exactly. On prom night, he went through two rolls of

film. He told my date to drive carefully, but the poor guy couldn't even see—"

"Who was your prom date? The first time, I mean."

"Scott Matheson."

Ethan arched an eyebrow. "That's a familiar name. Wasn't he—"

"The captain of the football team and an All-American," she said matter-of-factly, adding, "and you needn't look so surprised. I would have preferred that you were my date, but I wasn't pining away."

"Obviously not." He laughed ruefully and held his arm out for her. "Now that you've put me in my place, shall we go?"

Somehow, Ethan had managed to rent a small private conference room at the Nugget casino in Sparks. As promised, the room had been decorated in a nostalgic if slightly tacky style, reminiscent of a high school prom, with the noteworthy addition of multicolored lights and the ubiquitous revolving silver ball.

There was a five-member band, dressed in matching powder blue suits, probably purloined from one of the nostalgia shows in town. They were playing "My Girl" by the Temptations.

A table had been set up to one side of the room with a glass punchbowl, filled with what could only be 7-Up and red Hawaiian punch. There was also a silver tray of distinctly upscale cookies for refreshments. The only deviation from the formula was an ice bucket, in which was chilling a bottle of champagne.

Sydney was pleasantly surprised. Add an eagle-eyed chaperone standing watch at the door, and it wasn't far removed from the real deal. "This is for us?"

"Absolutely, our own private party. I didn't want to take a chance on having some punk football player cutting in on me."

"How did you arrange this?"

He shrugged. "I called in a favor or two from a friend of mine who's a high roller in town."

"I don't know what to say."

"Don't say anything." He leaned towards her and whispered in her ear, "Dance with me."

Sydney stepped into his arms without a word. Shivering slightly at the feel of his hand on her bare back, she rested her head on his shoulder and closed her eyes.

All the songs were slow songs. Time passed in slow motion as well, as the music segued between Smokey Robinson and the Miracles, to the Drifters, to Ben E. King, and even early Marvin Gaye and Al Green. It wasn't, strictly speaking, the music of her generation, but it didn't matter. It was timeless, and she surrendered to it.

Sydney could almost believe that she was sixteen again.

No wonder that the celebrants of Hot August Nights drove old cars and listened to Golden Oldies. It was a way of getting back to a simpler time. Of remembering when nothing mattered as much as being with the one person who made you feel like you'd never felt before—and would never feel again—if only because there could only be one first love.

There could only be one first kiss, ever.

And nothing would ever match the absolute devastation of that first heartbreak, the sense of overwhelming loss that threatened to eclipse the very sun, leaving the world in darkness.

Her own experience had been different simply because her heart belonged to Ethan, which rendered her immune to the charms of the boys her own age. There hadn't been anyone in junior high or high school who'd ignited a fever in her blood; although the hunky captain of the football team didn't know it, he never had a chance. She dated when the mood struck her, but always . . . indifferently.

Disinterest, of course, was a natural enticement, and there was usually some lovesick boy knocking at the door, to the dismay of her father and her mother's delight.

Her father needn't have worried.

"You're so quiet," Ethan whispered in her ear.

An hour had passed, or maybe more. "Am I?"

"To say the least. Tell me you're not bored."

"I'm not." Sydney pulled back so she could see his face. "I was remembering high school."

"But not Scott, I hope."

"Not Scott," she assured him.

"Good." His arm tightened around her. "I'm not keen on having competition."

"Ethan—"

"I know, there's Mitch," he said, his mouth near her ear. "But I'm not going to believe that until you walk down the aisle."

Sydney stopped dancing.

The music played on, another Temptations' classic, "Just My Imagination," sung soulfully by the band's drummer.

Ethan held her face in his hands and tilted her chin upward, so she couldn't turn away. "Don't marry him, Sydney. Not unless you're sure."

"But I am."

"Are you?"

"Ethan, I—"

He kissed her then, gently but firmly before hesitating, his mouth hovering a fraction of an inch above hers, his eyes searching for an answer.

Confused and inexplicably sad, Sydney drew back before he could kiss her again. Her pulse was racing, and she felt a little lightheaded. "This is wrong."

"Why?"

He knew the answer to that as well as she did, so she ignored the question. What he didn't know—and she couldn't bring herself to tell him—was that a lot had changed since April. "I think you'd better take me home."

They didn't speak during the drive back to the condo. The silence was almost palpable, taking the form of a nearly suffocating distance between them.

Although it bothered her, Sydney did not break the silence. There was nothing she could say that wouldn't be a betrayal of her feelings for Mitch. It had taken her years to make a commitment to him, but now that she had, she meant to honor it.

She blocked the thought from her mind and gazed out the window at the bright lights of Reno, a neon constellation of hot pink and deep purple.

Always the gentleman, Ethan walked her up the stairs to her front door. He held his hand out for the key and when she gave it to him, he unlocked the door.

"Thank you," she said, hating the meaningless sound of the words.

He returned the key. "Sydney, I need to know . . . have I ruined—"

"Please, let it go for tonight," she cut him off. "I can't think straight."

"All right," he said softly. "If you change your mind and want to talk, I'm staying at the Eldorado. I've got a seven-thirty flight back to San Diego in the morning, but you can call . . . anytime."

"Good night, Ethan." She started to close the door and hesitated, adding in all honesty, "I really had a lovely time."

"So did I."

It was nearly three A.M. before she fell into a restless sleep.

Sixteen

Saturday

Sydney was up to watch the sunrise. The pale morning sky imparted a curious sense of fragility and delicacy to the day, the light cool and soothing compared to that in the later part of the afternoon.

The air was fresh, scented with a hint of pine from the trees surrounding the condo. Across the way, someone had put up a feeder among a dozen or so hanging plants, and as she stood on the balcony, a Black-chinned hummingbird flitted back and forth from the trees to the feeder, time and again.

"Can't make up your mind either?" she asked.

The hummingbird evidently took offense at that and flew out of sight.

Sydney smiled and went inside. She gathered up the files she'd reviewed late last night when she couldn't sleep, and carried them downstairs.

Breakfast was a piece of peanut butter toast and a Pepsi, during which she finally finished reading the last of Xavier's reports. If indeed the murderer's identity was concealed within the files, she hadn't found it.

Yet.

All that remained was Laura's journal, and with any luck, she'd get to that tonight.

She also intended to work up a master time-line, an hour-

154

by-hour account in black and white of the day of the murders. Usually that was one of the first things she did in any case, but with years of paperwork to analyze and distill, something had to give.

"Tonight," she promised. "No more distractions."

Alan Foster showed up at nine A.M., virtually to the second.

At forty-two, Foster appeared to be aging precipitously, his hairline receding towards a bald pate. His plain wire-rimmed glasses suggested a disinterest in the ornamental, as did the lack of any other jewelry. He wore neither a ring nor a watch—odd given his precisely timed arrival—adding to the impression of unpretentiousness.

Although dressed casually in blue jeans and a polo shirt, he had the air of a man who was all business, all the time. Beneath that, Sydney sensed a certain watchfulness, as though he were assessing her—or more precisely, her reaction to him.

This was someone, she suspected, who micro-managed his life, fine-tuning his "performance" to create a very specific—if not necessarily accurate—image of himself. Observing him as he walked into the living room, sat and immediately adjusted his pant leg just so, she got the impression the man was a control freak.

"Now then," Alan Foster said, asserting that control, "what can I tell you that will help you catch my brother's killer?"

"That depends on what you know," Sydney answered, matching his abrupt tone. "Or what you're willing to tell me."

He drew his head back as if affronted, the light reflecting on his glasses effectively obscuring his eyes. "I have no secrets."

"I'm glad to hear that." She hadn't been taping the interviews thus far in the investigation, but instinct told her that

Foster would be more specific and thorough if he knew his statement was going to be transcribed word for word, so she turned on the cassette recorder. "Why don't you start by describing your relationship with Sean."

"We were very close," he said, a shade too quickly. "As I'm sure you know, our parents died when we were young. Even though our uncle took us in, I always felt like it was the two of us against the world."

"Were you happy living with your uncle?"

"Happy?" The initially quizzical expression on his face gave way to a frown. "I suppose we were, in a manner of speaking. We were together, at least. I remember hearing one of my aunts say that we might have to live apart, in separate homes—"

"When was that?"

"I don't know. It might have been the night of the . . . of our parents' funeral. The doctors weren't sure that Uncle Douglas was going to make it. My uncle was the executor of my parents' estate—and our legal guardian—so there was some confusion about what would happen if he should die."

"How old were you?"

"I was ten; Sean was seven."

Sydney couldn't keep herself from imagining how she would have felt in their situation; was there anything worse for a child than losing both parents at such a tender age? Knowing it was an understatement, she said, "That must have been a terrible shock."

Alan Foster stroked his chin, frowned again, and nodded thoughtfully. "A shock and something of a nightmare. I kept thinking, this can't really be happening. But it was. Sean got the worst of it, being so young. He was something of a mama's boy, you know, a sensitive little kid."

Which she took to mean Sean would have been more than

slightly upset if his brother had indeed tried to drown him, as Erin Cross contended. It was too early in their conversation to ask about the incident, however, so she let it pass. For now.

"But," Foster added flatly, "he got over it in due time. What they say about the resilience of youth is true in my experience. As unfortunate as our circumstances were, neither of us was scarred for life."

Sydney again reserved comment, doubting that he would admit or appreciate that his seemingly structured life might strike others as being totally joyless. Nor did she care to belabor the obvious, that Sean's life had been cut short by a bullet to the head. "Did the two of you remain close as you got older?"

"Yes, I would say so. The age difference became an issue when I turned thirteen—I didn't want him tagging after me, or hanging out with me and my friends—but it wasn't a major problem."

"What about in high school? Wasn't he a freshman during your senior year?"

"That's right."

"And presumably you had your driver's license and the use of a car?"

"Uncle Douglas allowed me to purchase a car when I turned sixteen," Foster admitted. "From the trust fund, you understand."

"Did you drive Sean to school?"

A flicker of annoyance showed in Foster's milky blue eyes. "Sometimes. Not always."

"Why not?"

He straightened his pant leg again although it didn't need it. "My brother had the unfortunate habit of being late on a regular basis. That was his choice, and I saw no need to make it my responsibility. If he wasn't ready when I was, I left without him."

"How did Sean react?"

"Well," Foster smiled grimly, "it obviously didn't cure him of being late."

"I hadn't heard there was a cure," she said, apropos of nothing. "What about after high school, when you were adults? I've been told both of you continued to live at your uncle's home."

"For awhile, yes."

"Was there any friction?"

"What there was, Ms. Bryant, was a difference in initiative. I signed up for some management courses at the university, and in short order had started my own business. Sean seemed to be waiting for inspiration to hit him between the eyes."

Like a bullet? It seemed an inappropriate turn of phrase under the circumstances, but she decided not to call him on it. "Were there other inspirations before the health spa?"

"No, the fat farm was the first. May I ask who told you about that?"

"Gary West mentioned it."

"Another dreamer," Foster said, and snorted derisively. "Talk about naiveté, squared. Their business plan was totally unrealistic, a bankruptcy waiting to happen. They would have gone under inside a year."

"How did you happen to see the business plan? West told me he hadn't finished writing it when Sean left for his honeymoon."

"I must have seen a draft." Foster shrugged. "Whatever, it was the most pitiful attempt at wishful thinking I've ever had the misfortune to read."

"Sean showed it to you?"

"No, he wouldn't have; he knew I'd tell him what I thought. Laura did. I assume she'd gotten it from Sean, but that's only supposition."

"Why bring it to you?"

"She valued my advice, even if my brother didn't."

"What did you tell her?"

"That no bank on the planet would fund a business loan for such an obvious white elephant. And if Sean used his own money, he'd be flat broke before he could cut the ribbon on opening day."

"Was she upset about it?"

Foster grimaced, tugging on his earlobe. "Wouldn't you be? It was Laura's future Sean was gambling with, as much as his own. She deserved better. A lot better."

Sydney wanted to get Alan Foster on record regarding his relationship with his brother's pretty young bride, so she asked, "Am I correct in assuming that—since she came to you for advice—the two of you were close?"

He hesitated, his forehead creasing into deep worry lines. "You do know that Laura and I dated before she ever met Sean."

"I've heard."

"I know some people found it strange that we remained friendly after the breakup, but the simple truth is, we had a lot in common."

"Such as?"

"An interest in the arts, primarily. Classical music, the opera . . ."

"Is that what you produce at your recording studio?" she asked. "Classical music?"

For some reason, the question made Foster seem ill at ease. He laughed nervously, as though embarrassed. "I wish that were the case, but unfortunately, we don't operate on that grand of a scale. My paying customers are mostly local groups. Amateur rock bands, country western singers, the occasional barbershop quartet."

"It sounds fascinating." Lightning did not strike her dead for the lie, for which she was grateful. "If a little off the subject. Back to Laura, if you don't mind. You said you remained friends?"

"Definitely."

"How did you feel, seeing her with your brother? The people I've talked to are of the opinion that you were in love with her."

"I won't deny that."

"It must have been painful to lose her to Sean. And watch her marry him."

"I wasn't happy about it, but I didn't have a choice in the matter."

For the moment Sydney couldn't think of a graceful way to phrase her next question, so she decided to come right out and ask. "Had you been lovers?"

"Yes," he said without hesitation. "If only briefly."

"So it was serious."

"For me it was. I brought her home to meet my family. In retrospect, not the best idea I ever had." Foster took off his glasses and wiped the lenses with a handkerchief he pulled from his pocket. "I wanted to marry her."

"Did you ask her?"

"I never got the chance." Eyes averted, he methodically polished his glasses. "One night I went to pick her up at her apartment, and found Sean there. It was obvious that they were . . . together."

Which wasn't quite how Douglas Foster had described it. "Was there a scene?"

"No. There might have been, except my little brother had

been drinking, and he'd passed out cold on her bed. It's not good form to confront a romantic rival who's dead to the world."

Another slip of the tongue? She wondered. "What did Laura say?"

"That she was sorry I had to find out that way. That she liked me very much, but there wasn't any real chemistry between us, and—"

"And you took it on the chin," Sydney finished for him, noting that his glasses were in danger of being shattered by too-vigorous cleaning. That betrayal by his brother and the woman he'd loved, coupled with the early loss of his parents, might very well account for his emotional retreat. Maybe his fear of being hurt again had robbed him of all feeling.

Or maybe he was seething inside.

"You must have been furious," she suggested.

Foster put his glasses on, finally, and looked directly at her, his lips drawn into a tight smile. "Are you perhaps inferring that I killed them?"

"Hadn't you tried to drown Sean when you were kids?"

Rather than being caught off-guard, his smile widened. "Now that you mention it, I believe I did. How did you hear about that? Wait, don't tell me. Erin. Am I right?"

She wasn't in the mood to answer questions, preferring to ask her own. "Why did you want to kill your brother?"

"Why would any kid want to get rid of a pesky little brother or sister?"

"You tell me; I'm an only child."

"Lucky you. He was bugging me and wouldn't shut up. He kept whining about how were we ever gonna find Mom and Dad in heaven. I figured I'd do him a favor and send him ahead, like a scout on 'Wagon Train.' So I pushed him under the water and held him there."

Sydney frowned. "Were you serious?"

"Yeah, for ten or fifteen seconds. Then I thought better of it . . . although I warned him if he told on me, they'd be fishing him off the bottom of the pool."

"You let him go?"

"Of course I let him go. Why? What did Erin say?"

She relayed Erin's version of events, that there had been a life-or-death struggle from which Sean broke free by kicking Alan in the chin.

"What a crock," Foster snapped, narrowing his eyes. "That never happened, except in Sean's dreams. Leave it to my baby brother to lie like a bandit to make himself look good . . . or me look bad."

Knowing from the outset that there was no way for her to verify whose version of the incident was the truth, Sydney concentrated on gauging Foster's reaction. That he appeared angry surprised her a little, given the manner in which he held his emotions in check. It did prove, however, that he had a temper. And he was presumably capable of violence. That revelation alone was worth the price of admission.

"All right." Having found a chink in his armor, she persisted: "Tell me what you remember about your brother's wedding day."

"Whew." Foster exhaled noisily. "What I remember? Has anyone been able to recount that day in any detail?"

"You'd be amazed at what people remember." In fact, she'd never worked a case where the witnesses recalled so many of the details. Of course, they all had given statements to the police back then; having "gone on the record" undoubtedly reinforced those memories now. "Did you dance with Laura?"

"Yes."

"And you kissed the bride?"

He nodded, his expression pensive. "Isn't that traditional? We all did; Uncle Douglas, Randy of course, and even Gary."

"Did you talk with Sean before they left for their honeymoon?"

"I . . . no. There was really nothing to say. I'm not enough of a hypocrite to pretend I was happy that he'd taken my girl. I shook his hand as they were getting ready to leave—late as usual—but that's all."

"And Laura? Did you speak to her?"

Foster shook his head. "I wish now that I had."

"Where did you go after the reception?"

"Down to the studio."

That agreed with the statement he'd given to the police. Knowing what the answer should be, she tested him by asking, "Did you see anyone there?"

"I made it a point not to see anyone. I went in the back way, went straight to my office, locked myself in . . . and the world out."

"How long were you there?"

"Until about eight o'clock. I did some paperwork, listened to a couple of demo tapes, checked the schedule to see who'd booked studio time for the coming week, and then took a nap. There's a couch in my office, and I needed to sleep off the champagne."

So far, his story matched. It also sounded remarkably well rehearsed. "What kind of a car were you driving?" she asked, hoping to break his rhythm.

"I had a Jaguar XKE."

A Jag wouldn't stand a chance off-road, Sydney knew. "Was that your only car?"

He smiled fractionally. "I couldn't afford a second car and make the payments on my Jag, trust fund or not."

"How about a motorcycle?"

163

"A motorcycle," he said, as if taken aback at the very thought. "Do I look like a biker to you?"

He didn't, even remotely, but a lot of time had passed. "Is that a no?"

"No, I did not own, borrow, *or* steal a motorcycle."

The tape in the recorder clicked loudly just then, and Sydney leaned forward to turn the cassette over. After pressing the record button, she looked up to find Foster watching her intently. "Is something wrong?"

"To be candid, yes. I've made an honest effort to answer your questions, regardless of how humiliating I found them to be. Now I have a question for you."

"Go ahead."

"Uncle Douglas tells me you're operating on the assumption that whoever murdered Sean and Laura was at the house that day."

"That's right."

"Am I a suspect?"

Sydney didn't answer, but instead looked him straight in the eye. She noticed his brow furrow and saw a hint of a twitch near the corner of his right eye. Even so, he held her gaze, never blinking. A minute passed in silence. The only sound was the quiet hum of the recorder.

"I haven't decided," she said finally, searching his face for a crack in the facade of his control. "Did you do it?"

"No."

"Do you know who did?"

"No."

"Any suspicions?"

"Off the record?"

"If you prefer."

Foster's quick intake of breath suggested he was bracing himself. He covered his mouth with his hand—trying to hold the words in?—and then shook his head resolutely.

"Randy had a motorcycle," he said. "He was riding it that day."

Seventeen

"Do you know where I can find him?" Sydney asked. Douglas Foster had given her a phone number for Randy Leighton, but there was never an answer when she called.

"Randy? My guess is he's . . . working."

"Where does he work?"

"Oh, here in town, at a bar called Smokey's."

"He's a bartender?" She had developed an aversion to bartenders, since a particularly loathsome accumulation of primordial ooze by the name of Joey tried to assault her a few months back.

"Not exactly." Foster reprised his tight-lipped smile. "But you'll see. Smokey's is a quiet little dive fifty-one weeks out of the year, but during Hot August Nights, the place is packed with tourists."

Just what she needed. "Would you mind giving me directions?"

Smokey's Bar & Grill was located in a strip mall off of California Avenue, between a Mail Boxes Etc. and a store that sold used women's clothing on consignment, called Wear Ever You Go.

The parking lot resembled an open-air auto museum. Proud drivers protected their investments from the blazing sun by erecting portable canopies over their cars. A few shared the shade with their vehicles, sitting in beach chairs and sipping beer. Others, though, seemed to work steadily even in the stifling heat, dusting and polishing their treasures.

As she made her way towards Smokey's from where she'd parked near the street, Sydney identified a classic or two, starting with a 1954 Buick Riviera, painted tangerine orange, its interior a pristine white. And she noticed a 1958 Ford Edsel, its trademark grill gleaming in the sun, with a custom paint job that had the front of the car black, lightening to blue at the rear.

Inside, the upholstery was black leather, and the steering wheel was made out of silver handcuffs, welded together with thick links of chain. The Idaho license plate read, B Not T.

Be naughty, on a black-and-blue car. Obviously not all of the Fifties crowd was as conservative as their decade of choice. Smiling and shaking her head, she pushed open the heavy wood door to the bar and stepped inside.

True to its name, Smokey's had limited visibility due to a cloud of smoke that swirled indolently in the backwash from a row of ceiling fans. The place smelled of cigarette smoke and the yeasty scent of tap beer.

The hardwood floor was littered with sawdust shavings and peanut shells, and a scattering of popcorn. There was a four foot tall barrel full of peanuts at the near end of the bar, and a fully operational popcorn machine to the left of the cash register. Plastic baskets were stacked nearby, for the customers to serve themselves.

There were high-backed booths lining the walls, plus a dozen or so round wooden tables in the open floor. Wood captain's chairs surrounded each table; virtually every seat was taken.

Towards the back was a game room, dominated by a regulation-size pool table. There were also dartboards on the walls, and several bulky video game machines in the far corner. The jukebox was playing Pat Boone's dreamy "Love Letters In The Sand" loud enough to rattle the windows, if there'd been any to rattle.

Sydney had only a general description of Randy Leighton— Alan Foster described his cousin as being five foot eight, with a medium build, and brown hair—which probably fit ten to twenty percent of the males in the room. She went to the bar and caught the eye of the sixtyish bartender, who nodded and ambled over to her, wiping his hands on the towel looped through his apron tie.

"Can I help you?" he yelled over the din.

"I'm looking for Randy Leighton. Do you know where I might find him?"

The bartender turned to look in the direction of the game room, then pointed. "You see that guy chalking his cue? The one in the black shirt? That's Randy."

"Thanks."

"My pleasure," the bartender said and winked. "Only take my advice, young lady, and don't let him con you into shooting pool."

"Don't worry," she said, "I'm not interested in playing games."

Her mother would have said Randy Leighton was as cute as a button, whatever that meant. He had dark, curly hair, eyes as blue as the Nevada sky, and dark eyelashes that most women would envy. His smile was on the crooked side, a little shy but engaging.

He had a swimmer's build, his arms tan and leanly muscled without the bulk of someone who lifted weights. His black shirt was in fact made of see-through mesh, revealing a hard, flat abdomen with only a trace of dark hair at the navel.

Leighton was drawing, Sydney noticed, a fair amount of attention from the females in the bar, some plainly inviting while others—those with male companions—cast covert glances when the opportunity arose. She noticed, too, that she was getting some less than friendly looks from both camps as she approached him.

Like she needed another man in her life.

"Hi," Leighton said before she could introduce herself. "Hot, isn't it?"

"Very." She extended her hand, intent upon establishing that her reason for being here was strictly business. "My name is Sydney Bryant, Mr. Leighton—"

"Randy."

"—and I'm working for Douglas Foster, investigating your cousin Sean's death."

"Right, I heard." His handshake was firm, his gaze direct. "That was something, finding a skull after all these years."

"Is there somewhere private we could talk?"

"Private?" He leaned over the pool table to line up his shot. The cue's hard rubber tip came to within a millimeter of the white cue ball before he drew his arm back, paused, and hit a quick, clean shot that split the nine and four balls, sinking them in opposite corner pockets. "I guess that could be arranged."

"It won't take long."

"Doesn't matter." He smiled, breaking down his cue and putting it in a blue velvet-lined case. "There's not much action till late afternoon, and I really don't need the practice."

"Are you the resident pool shark?" she asked, noting that the clasps and handle on the case appeared to be made of finely-etched silver.

"More like a guppy." Leighton laughed. "Come on, we

can talk in Art's office. You want something to drink? A beer or maybe a Coke?"

"Pepsi, if you have it." Sydney followed him, weaving among the tables, aware that she was the subject of a number of envious looks.

Leighton ducked behind the bar and opened a huge cooler filled with crushed ice. Digging in the ice, he extracted a couple of bottles of Corona beer and a can of Pepsi. He popped the caps off the beer and spoke briefly to the bartender, gesturing towards a side door.

The song on the jukebox changed to "April Love," also sung by Pat Boone in a style conducive to well-mannered swooning.

"Follow me," Randy Leighton said a moment later, handing her the icy can.

Art's office was located down a narrow hall towards the back of the building. It was almost claustrophobically small, perhaps eight feet by eight feet, and crowded with a desk, two metal filing cabinets, and floor-to-ceiling shelves stacked with boxes of booze.

The usual suspects were in evidence: Johnnie Walker, Jack Daniel's, and Jim Beam, among others.

"So," Leighton said, sitting on a corner of the desk. "What do you want to know?"

"First off, how old were you in 1985?"

"Seventeen."

"And how are you related to Sean?"

"Our mothers were sisters." He took a swig of beer. "Mom was the youngest, and she didn't marry as well as Aunt Rachel, but the two of them were pretty tight. Which is why, after my aunt was killed, Mom did her best to stay in touch with Sean and Alan."

Sydney had read the names of Rachel and Patrick Foster in the newspaper clipping describing their fatal accident in 1968, but this was the first time she'd heard either name spoken aloud. It was a poignant reminder that every life touched other lives, and every death represented a loss to many. "What about the rest of the family?"

Leighton put his thumb over the top of the beer bottle, shook it slightly, then let it foam into his mouth. After a moment, he shook his head. "Not so you'd notice, but there are reasons why they didn't. Maybe not the best reasons, but reasons."

It was definitely off the subject, but she was curious about the other side of Sean's family. "Such as?"

"Such as people were bent out of shape that Aunt Rachel didn't name them in her will. They figured she got stuck up or something, forgot her roots."

"Did she have any money of her own?"

"No, but she was insured. Mom told me that there was probably a couple of hundred thousand dollars' worth of life insurance, with double indemnity for accidental death. Could have been as much as half a million bucks. The relatives figured maybe they'd get some of that, but Aunt Rachel left it all in trust for her boys."

"Sounds responsible to me."

"Except . . . no one in our family ever had two dimes to rub together, and I guess when they heard about the insurance, they got to dreaming about what it could buy. There were some pretty hard feelings."

"Still, how can they blame her for looking out for her kids?"

"That's just it. Uncle Patrick had already provided for the boys. He left them more than enough to be raised proper and go to college."

"Even so—"

"My mom says the question at the time was, why not spread the wealth? Of course, I wasn't even born when all this happened, so it's no skin off my nose that I wasn't mentioned in the will."

Sydney did the math in her head. "Your mother was pregnant when her sister was killed?"

"Seven months along. As a matter of fact, they were headed for Austin to visit my mom when the accident happened. You know Austin?"

"Afraid not; I'm from California."

"I thought so. You don't look like a native, that's for sure. Austin's my hometown, but it's way out in the middle of nowhere, in a state that's got a *lot* of nowhere. Getting there from anywhere takes some doing."

"Via an isolated stretch of road," she said, recalling how the newspaper had described the accident site.

"It is that. Anyway, they had a trunk-load of baby gifts for my mom. And me, I guess. I'm not sure why Douglas came with them, unless maybe Aunt Rachel planned to do a little matchmaking."

"Matchmaking?"

He nodded. "My father ran out on my mother when he heard she was expecting me. He joined the Army and was stationed in Germany when I was born. He died in a helicopter crash when I was two years old."

"I'm sorry."

"Shit happens," he said philosophically. "You gotta carry on. The point is, Mom saw to it that I knew my cousins. I don't know that Sean and Alan were thrilled to have a snot-nosed kid underfoot, but I spent a couple of summers at the house."

"Were you staying there in the summer of 1985?"

"Yep." Leighton took another swig of beer. "It was cool,

though. I had my bike and wasn't dependent on anyone to get around."

"You all got along?"

"Sure did."

"And you knew Laura?"

"Of course."

"Did you like her?"

He smiled. "I liked her a lot."

Looking at him, Sydney was glad they hadn't tried to talk in the bar; that shy, sweet, killer smile might have incited a riot among the female patrons of Smokey's. "How much is a lot?"

"Well . . . you gotta remember, I was seventeen. I don't mean to be crude, but I was pretty much in a constant state of arousal. Laura was gorgeous, sexy, and she really liked to flirt."

"She flirted with you?"

"All the time."

"Was it serious?"

"I don't know. We never were alone together for more than a few minutes. I never made a pass at her, if that's what you're asking."

"Was Sean aware of the situation?"

"He wasn't blind."

She took that as a yes. "Did he ever say anything to you about it?"

"Not really." Leighton finished off the first beer, placed the bottle on its side on the desk blotter, and gave it a spin. With an impish grin, he added, "But . . . I could tell he was a little jealous."

"Did Laura know?"

"Don't women always know?"

"Probably. Okay, so tell me about the wedding reception," she said, watching the bottle's lazy spin, "when you and Laura danced."

"It really wasn't a big deal. I've always liked to dance, and people tell me I'm pretty good at it. I can watch someone do a routine and pick it up—" he snapped his fingers "—just like that."

Sydney had a hunch that he never lacked for willing partners.

"Anyway, Laura had stage experience as a dancer, so she was good at it, too. One of her favorite songs came on; I can't remember what it was, but give me a minute, it'll come to me. She wanted to dance, but Sean had been drinking, as usual."

"So she asked you?"

"Actually, she didn't say a word. She just turned and looked at me."

"Go on."

"I got up and came over to her, and we started dancing. Wait, I remember the song. 'Gypsy Woman.' You know it?"

"I think I do."

"It's kind of . . . sensuous. Sultry. Drums and violins get my blood up, if you know what I mean."

Sydney smiled faintly.

"I suppose I should have known better, but Laura kind of melted into me, and I kind of forgot there was anyone else in the room. We were so close, I could feel her heartbeat."

"That must have been some dance."

"I could show you," he offered, standing up. "It was hot!"

"Thanks, I'll take your word for it."

"Are you sure?" A smile played at the corners of his mouth. "I think you'd like it."

Sydney felt her color rise. "I think you're right, but I'm all danced out."

"Okay, but if you change your mind . . ." He executed an

effortless turn, did a few steps ending with a ball change and sat down with a flourish. "I'm ready."

She got the distinct impression that the invitation had little to do with dancing. "What happened next?"

He shrugged. "Sean flipped out. He grabbed me and spun me around. I thought he was gonna take a swing at me, but Laura stepped between us."

"Did he say anything?"

"Oh yeah." The muscles in his jaw tightened. "He said, 'Keep your white trash hands off my wife.' "

"What did you do?"

"Nothing. He had forty pounds on me, besides being half in the tank. I told him I didn't mean anything by it, and I tried to apologize, but that seemed to make him madder, God only knows why."

"What did Laura do?"

"She was cooing at him, trying to pull him away. Then he reached around her and gave me a shove, hard enough that I stumbled backwards and almost fell." He made a face, as if the memory pained him. "I started after him, but Gary grabbed Sean and Alan took hold of me. That put an end to it."

"Did you say anything to Sean?"

For the first time, Leighton hesitated before answering. "Knowing me, I guess so. I didn't appreciate being called white trash, I can tell you that."

"You don't remember what you said?"

"Not really." He frowned. "Why? Has somebody told you otherwise?"

Nobody had, but based on his hesitation, she decided to bluff. "There are a couple of versions, actually. I talked to Alan just this morning—"

"Yeah, like he's not biased."

Sydney looked him straight in the eyes. "Everyone is biased, Randy. What I do as an investigator is listen to eight or nine different versions of what happened that day, and sort it all out."

"Meaning what?"

"Meaning I'd like to hear it from you. No matter what you said, I want to hear it from you. If you remember."

"Damn." He ran a hand through his hair and looked away, his right leg bouncing, as though he was stricken with a sudden case of nerves. "I remember . . . it wasn't nice."

"What?"

He hesitated, his expression troubled. "I said, 'Touch me again and I'll kill you, you sorry son of a bitch.' "

Eighteen

"That's certainly direct and unambiguous," Sydney said, wondering why no one had mentioned it to her before now. "Were you serious?"

"I was mad," Leighton said. "He insulted my mother. Drunk or not, he had no call. But we both cooled down, and that was all there was to it."

"No hard feelings?"

"Not on my part. I may be hot-headed on occasion, but I've never been one to hold a grudge."

She didn't point out that he wouldn't have had to hold it for very long, since Sean Foster was dead within a matter of hours. "Did you talk to him afterwards?"

"No. Under the circumstances, I thought it best to keep my distance."

"Did you talk to Laura?"

"For a minute, yeah. I'd gone down to the pool and she came looking for me."

"What did she say?"

"That it was all her fault, and she was sorry Sean took it out on me. She told me she hated it when Sean drank too much, especially after he'd promised her he would try to go easy on the sauce."

"Anything else?"

"She said she was going to have her hands full, straightening him out—"

Sydney frowned. "Was that also in reference to his drinking?"

"I'm not sure; she was upset and talking a blue streak, but not everything she said made sense. I remember something about picking up the dry cleaning, something about how it was high time for the Lone Ranger to kiss Tonto good-bye."

"Meaning?"

"That's just it, I have no idea. I'm not even sure she knew what she was saying. There were quite a few champagne toasts throughout the afternoon; she might have been plastered herself."

"Lovely," Sydney said under her breath.

"Anyway, that's pretty much all there was to it. Tiki showed up maybe thirty seconds later, and the two of them started whispering and giggling about some girl thing. I went back inside."

"How well did you know Tiki Everly?"

"Well enough to realize the lady was a few cherries short of a jubilee," he drawled and grinned engagingly. "Why do you ask?"

"I need to talk to her, but so far no one's been able to find her." The last fax she'd gotten from the office had again listed "no progress" next to the elusive Ms. Everly's name.

"You're kidding, right?"

"Unfortunately, I'm not," Sydney said. "We've checked the Department of Motor Vehicles in California and Nevada, national directory services, voter registration records—"

Randy Leighton laughed. "No wonder. Tiki doesn't drive, her phone isn't listed in her name, and as for voting, I doubt she'd want to risk the bad karma that voting for the wrong person would bring."

"I take it you know where she is?"

"Sure. I run into her now and then around town. She's got a little house off of 5th Street. It's a fortune telling parlor; she lives in the back."

"Tiki is a fortune teller?"

He nodded. "Weird, isn't it? She's even got a crystal ball. From what I hear, she's pretty good at it. I don't remember the address, it's either on Vine or Washington, I think. Or it might be on Ralston, I suppose. But you can't miss the house; there's this big ugly plastic eyeball hanging over the front door, the better to see into the future with, I guess."

"How is she with the past?"

"That I don't know." He did a little drumbeat on his thighs. "So are we finished? Because I'd like to take you to—"

"Almost," she cut him off, "but not quite. Where did you go after the reception?"

"I headed back to Austin on my bike."

Which of course would be all but impossible to prove or disprove. "If you were spending the summer in Reno, why the trip home?"

"I don't know. I was feeling kind of restless. Don't you ever get the urge to just say the hell with it, and take off?"

"Occasionally, but I get over it."

This time his smile was subversive. "You don't know what you're missing."

"How far," she persisted, "is it to Austin?"

"A hundred sixty, maybe a hundred seventy miles, give or take."

"What's that translate to in driving time? Three or four hours?"

"Depends upon who's driving. I've made the trip in a little over two hours riding at night, you know, full throttle, throwing caution to the wind. Or you can mosey along like somebody's great-grandmama and stretch it out to five."

"What about that night?"

"Your guess is as good as mine. I know I was home when Mom got in around midnight." His expression changed to one of mild amusement. "Kind of pathetic, don't you think? To be seventeen on a Saturday night, sitting alone watching 'War of the Worlds,' waiting up for my mother to come in from a hot date."

"Yes, well I can tell it's arrested your social development," she said, not bothering to disguise her skepticism. "I don't suppose you saw or talked to anyone that evening? A neighbor or a friend?"

"Not even the neighbor's cat. I did stop in Fallon for gas and to, you know, wash up. But I doubt if anyone would have remembered me, even back then, as busy as it gets on a weekend night."

"Ergo, you don't have an alibi."

"Ergo is right. That would be helpful, wouldn't it? If everyone but the killer had an alibi?"

"It would make my job easier," she agreed, even though she had worked cases in which purportedly ironclad alibis had vaporized in the light of day.

"But you know—" he stood up and stretched lazily, raising his arms over his head, exposing his flat tanned belly "—if I were planning to murder somebody, I would go out of my way to make sure I had some kind of an alibi. I mean, the fact that I don't have one seems to me to be proof of innocence."

"It doesn't usually work that way." Sydney glanced at her watch; it was a quarter past twelve. "One last question and I'll let you get back to work. Do you now have or have you ever had any suspicion as to who might have killed Sean and Laura?"

He didn't answer immediately, but sat down, lacing his

fingers together around his right knee. A minute or two passed in silence, and then he sighed. "I think the police were right."

That wasn't what she'd expected to hear.

"I can't really explain why, but . . . nothing else makes any sense."

"There's a lot of that going around," Sydney observed wryly as she got to her feet. "Particularly in this case. Anyway, thank you for your cooperation; I've taken enough of your time."

Leighton stood; in the tight confines of the office, they were only inches apart. "Why don't you let me take you to lunch?"

"I really can't. I'd like to talk to Tiki Everly today, if possible."

"Well, how about we have lunch and then I'll show you where she lives?"

"Sorry, I'm on a tight schedule." Which wasn't exactly true, but he didn't need to know that. She took a half step backwards, at the same time extending her hand in what she hoped was a cool and professional manner. "And I'm already running late."

"Okay, I don't want to hold you up." Randy Leighton smiled in apparent resignation and shook her hand, holding it perhaps a fraction of a second longer than necessary. "You can reach me here if you have any other questions. Or if you change your mind about . . . lunch."

Traffic in downtown Reno nearly rivaled L.A. for gridlock, the streets overflowing with classic cars and an astonishing number of people who jaywalked with impunity. Sandwiched between a Kiwi-colored Plymouth sedan with a license plate that read Spor T 40, and a 1962 Chevrolet Impala SuperSport painted peppermint pink, Sydney kept an eye on the Probe's thermostat as she inched her way along Virginia Street.

She made a left on 5th Street, finally escaping the low-speed parade, and within a few minutes was cruising Vine, looking for the aforementioned eyeball.

The house so adorned was a single-story, wood frame bungalow with peeling white paint. It sat on a weed-choked lot, enclosed by a chain-link fence. There was a separate garage to the right of the house, with barn-style doors that had to be opened by hand.

The doors were in fact open, revealing a workshop of sorts. Standing at a high table in the center of the garage was a gray-haired woman who appeared to be in her seventies, wearing safety goggles and blue mechanic's overalls. There were two huge oscillating fans in the back, standing like sentinels against the heat.

Sydney pulled into the driveway, parked and got out of the car.

"Hello," the woman called, waving. She pushed the goggles up as she came from the shaded garage into the bright afternoon sun. "My Lord, but it's hot as the dickens, isn't it?"

"Definitely."

"I think it's going to storm tonight," the woman went on, looking to the west where thunderheads were massing over the mountains. "If it does, I'm going to take off my shoes and play in the puddles."

Thirty seconds in the direct sun and Sydney could already feel the sweat beading on her forehead. "That sounds like a plan."

"If I was younger," the woman confided, lowering her voice to just above a whisper, "I'd take off my clothes, too, but I wouldn't want to spook the animals or frighten any small children who might happen by."

"I wouldn't worry about it," Sydney said with a smile, then introduced herself. "I'd like to talk to Tiki Everly, if that's possible."

"It's certainly possible, but it isn't likely," the woman said. "I'm Hortensia, Tiki's godmother. I'm afraid she's gone for the afternoon."

Somehow, that didn't come as a surprise. "When do you expect her back?"

"Oh, dinner time, I would imagine. Or you could go over to Lawlor Events Center; she's helping a friend sell T-shirts for Hot August Nights."

"Would she have time to talk to me?"

"I have no idea." Hortensia took a handkerchief out of the coveralls and dabbed at her face. "Saturday is probably the busiest day. And I know the parking situation over there can be dreadful . . ."

Even so, Sydney thought she might as well try. As the final wedding party guest and Laura's friend, Tiki could hold the key to unlocking the mystery of what had happened that night. Or not. Either way, the questions had to be raised. "Where is Lawlor Event Center?"

"I'll show you," Hortensia said. "Come with me."

Sydney followed her into the garage—past the table on which the older woman had been cutting colored glass to make a stained glass window—to the back wall where an over-sized city map had been mounted.

Hortensia peered at the map for a moment before tapping her finger on the paper. "We're right here. The quickest way from here to Lawlor is to take 5th back to Virginia and make a left." She traced her finger slowly along the route in illustration. "Cross over the freeway and you'll see the university to the right. Lawlor is on the campus, a little bit further on, also on the right."

"Got it."

"Now I'm giving you fair warning, the crowd can be as thick as ticks on a bloodhound. Most of the parking lots are roped off, used for showing the cars, but somewhere among all of that, you'll find several booths selling event souvenirs. And beer, for those foolhardy enough to partake of spirits under the midday sun."

Sydney smiled, taken with Hortensia's old-fashioned turn of phrase. "Would you mind describing Tiki for me, since we've never met?"

"Describe Tiki? Well, she's petite, about five feet tall, if that, and slight of build. If you saw her from the back, you might think she was twelve."

Remembering Douglas Foster's account of her quixotic sense of style and mindful of the fact that Ms. Everly told fortunes for a living, she asked, "Do you recall what was she wearing today?"

"Goodness," Hortensia fretted, "this is like reporting a missing person, isn't it?"

"Except Tiki isn't missing."

"Thank heavens! But let's see . . . I believe she had on a purple peasant skirt, and a turquoise shirt she bought at the Indian colony. You wouldn't think purple and turquoise would go together, but they do."

At least Tiki Everly should stand out in a crowd, Sydney thought. She dug in the back pocket of her jeans for a business card and handed it to Hortensia. "If I miss her, would you have her call me this evening? My local number is on the back there."

"Oh my! You're a private investigator? Tiki's not in any trouble, is she?"

"Not at all, but I do need to talk to her."

Hortensia's eyes widened. "Is this about the girl who got murdered?"

"You know about that?"

"Not to speak of, although . . . Tiki said the other morning that the time was coming when the truth would finally be told . . . and the dead would be at peace."

Nineteen

Hortensia's warning about parking at Lawlor Event Center proved to be warranted. Sydney cruised the campus twice, to no avail. As she waited in the left turning lane for a third circuit, she noticed campus police were erecting barricades at the Virginia Street entrance, complete with signs reading "All Lots Full."

"I can take a hint," she said. Rather than making a futile turn, she merged back into the traffic lane and headed for the condo.

If she didn't hear from Tiki Everly by eight o'clock, she would make a return trip to the house off 5th Street this evening. If Tiki wasn't home, she'd try again first thing in the morning. And she would keep going back until she got the interview.

In the interim, she would finish reading Laura Clifford Foster's journal, do the time-line, and perhaps take a catnap to make up for missing sleep.

And she would call Mitch. She felt that she had to tell him about Ethan's visit; trust was an elemental part of their relationship, and she wasn't comfortable with the idea of violating it. More than that, she wanted to hear his voice. Maybe even *needed* to.

There was a green and white patrol car parked in front of the condo, the word Sheriff painted across the trunk. As she waited for the garage door to open, she saw a uniformed officer come from around the far side of the building, his posture and bearing suggestive of someone with a military background.

Sydney pulled into the garage and parked. A glance in her rearview mirror confirmed that the deputy was standing at parade rest near the door.

He appeared to be in his early fifties, tanned and fit at approximately five foot ten. His black hair was frosted with silver at the temples, his gaze uncompromising under thick eyebrows that slanted downward as though frozen in a perpetual frown, over features stern enough to have been carved from stone.

"Are you Cindy Bryant?" he asked as she stepped from the car. "The private investigator?"

"Sydney," she corrected. "I am."

"I'm Frank Micelli," he said, and nodded curtly. "I heard you were working on the Foster homicides. I was in charge of the police investigation."

He seemed to be waiting for acknowledgment, so she said, "Yes, I know."

"You probably also know the case is closed, but I thought we should talk."

Her instinct was that he really meant he should talk, and she should shut up and listen. As unappealing as that prospect was, she was a little curious about what the man had to say. "Then come in."

Micelli followed her up the stairs and stood waiting, hands behind his back, as she struggled briefly with the door lock, which again wanted to stick.

"A little WD-40 would clear that right up," Micelli noted.

"I'll advise the management," she said, wiggling the key to free it from the lock.

"The only reason I mention it is that a gummy lock is a potential security risk. Imagine trying to unlock this door with someone after you—"

Given his paternalistic tone and her suspicion that there was an unspoken but condescending "little lady" echoing in his head, Sydney had to work at a smile. "As I said, I'll take care of it."

"Just trying to help."

"And I appreciate it." She reached to push the button engaging the automatic garage door, then went inside, Micelli hot on her heels. She walked into the kitchen, hoping that he would respect her boundaries and stay on the other side of the breakfast bar.

He did, standing rigidly as if at attention, all the while scanning the room.

Looking for security risks, she thought. "I'm sorry I don't have coffee, but can I offer you a glass of ice water or a Pepsi?"

"Water's fine."

She got the bucket of ice cubes from the freezer and filled a tall glass, adding water from the tap. Grabbing a Pepsi for herself, she returned to the bar and handed Micelli the glass.

"Thanks." Belatedly, he pulled out a stool and sat down, placing his hat on the bar. "I understand you're from California?"

"San Diego."

A corner of his mouth quirked into an imitation of a smile. "Couldn't find enough work in a city that big to keep you at home?"

Which wasn't exactly "Welcome to Nevada," but rather than giving Micelli the satisfaction of knowing he'd annoyed her, she simply smiled and said, "I prefer the challenge of working on cases the police can't solve . . . like the Foster murders."

"The case is closed, Ms. Bryant. Officially."

"So I've heard. I'm sure you realize, however, that closing a case and solving a case are not necessarily one and the same. My client isn't satisfied with your conclusions, however 'official' they might be."

"I suppose if your client wants to waste his money," Micelli shrugged, "that's his privilege. But you're wasting your time."

"That's my concern." She popped the top of her Pepsi and took a sip, looking at him steadily over the rim of the can. "Is that what you came to talk about? If it is, you're the one who's wasting my time."

Irritation flared in his eyes, even as he laughed, feigning amusement. "Don't take it personally, Ms. Bryant; I'm only trying to help."

"Obviously."

"If it turns out that you're right and I'm wrong, I'll be the first to congratulate you, one law enforcement professional to another."

But don't hold your breath, she thought.

"In the meantime, I heard that you had expressed an interest in our unsuccessful attempts to locate the murder weapon."

Based on what Jim Wagner had to say about Micelli and his Personality Deficit Disorder, she doubted he would have spoken to his former partner. "Who told you that?"

"Word gets around. The point is, the fact that we were unable to find the weapon proves virtually nothing. It is *not* evidence of Sean Foster's innocence, regardless of what his uncle chooses to believe."

"You'll excuse me if I disagree."

"Disagree all you want, that doesn't change the cold, hard facts. That's one hell of a big desert out there, and even if the

189

department had the inclination, the money, and the manpower to conduct a wider search—which we don't—the outcome would more than likely be the same. You've got to factor in the probability that in fifteen years, the boy's skull may have washed who knows how many miles from where he killed himself—"

"Or was shot."

"Get real!" Micelli scoffed, his tone contemptuous. "My guess is that the only proof Douglas Foster would accept as definitive that Sean committed suicide is finding his nephew's skeletonized hand still clutching the gun. Which ain't gonna happen."

"Can you blame him for wanting proof? Is he supposed to accept Sean's guilt based entirely on supposition? Because that's what it comes down to, doesn't it? The police have a theory and not a damned thing more."

"And what do you have, Ms. Bryant?"

It was clearly a taunt; discretion kept her from answering in kind. "I don't think you can eliminate the possibility that no one ever found either the knife or the gun for the simple reason that the killer took them with him."

"In which case, searching for them would be a waste of time."

Sydney had already come to that conclusion on her own, although she didn't care to admit that to Micelli. "Unless someone found the rest of the bones—"

"Not if the coyotes got to him. His remains could be scattered for miles."

"Still—"

"Look, you're trying to prove a negative. The absence of either weapon is a non-starter. We both know defendants are convicted every day without the police ever finding the murder weapon."

"That may be true, but—"

"But nothing. If you're so sure somebody's gotten away with murder, prove it."

Unfortunately, he was right. Her theories about the case were no more valid than his without documentation and/or testimony to back them up. What frustrated her was that after four days of investigation, and having talked to all but the last witness, she had yet to come across anything that would qualify as hard evidence.

"Wasn't there ever a moment," she tried one last time, "when you wondered if you were mistaken? If you might have missed something?"

"Not then and not now."

"And if you're wrong? What if there's a killer walking free today because you missed a vital piece of evidence?"

"That isn't likely." Micelli stood up, straightened his shoulders and reached for his hat. "In all these years, I've never found one iota of evidence that Sean Foster didn't kill his bride, for the simple reason that it doesn't exist. It never has."

"How do you know if you never looked?"

"Take my word for it. The kid was drunk, he was wildly jealous, and he was there. That makes him three for three in my book."

Sydney would bet the farm there was only a single page in Deputy Frank Micelli's book. "Thanks for stopping by," she said, not bothering to sound sincere. "I'll show you to the door."

"I can find my way out. Good day," Micelli said, with a tip of his hat. Leather creaked as he hitched up his belt and strode out of the kitchen.

She stayed where she was, both hands braced on the counter, until she heard the front door slam shut. Then she closed her eyes and leaned over until her forehead rested on the cool ceramic tile.

"Save me," she muttered.

There was no answer when she tried to call Mitch at home, so she dialed his direct line at the police department. The phone rang a dozen times before he answered.

"Travis," he said, sounding out of breath.

"I thought you had the day off."

"I do, can't you tell?" His voice lost its hard, big-city edge. "Only I got so damned lonely, I came in to catch up on my paperwork. If the city keeps raining new forms on us, I'm going to have to rent a bulldozer to clear my desk."

Sydney laughed, tucking her legs beneath her on the futon. "You have my utmost sympathy."

"Hmm. There are other things I'd rather have."

"Behave yourself, Lieutenant."

"Like I have a choice, with you out of state. Speaking of which, how's your investigation going?"

"It could be better." She sighed and gave him an abbreviated account of the past few days, ending with the highlights of her encounter with Micelli.

"So you pissed off another deputy," Mitch said when she finished. "I can't say I'm surprised; you do seem to have a talent for that."

"Evidently. Suffice it to say, I won't be speeding on county roads anytime soon."

"Is he that mad?"

"Not mad, exactly, but I think Deputy Micelli would be delighted to give me a guided tour of the jail, including an overnight stay."

"Well, watch your back."

"I always do."

"And call me if you need bailing out."

"Don't worry, I will." She hesitated, thinking how best to bring up the subject of Ethan's visit, when she heard loud voices in the background over the phone.

"Sydney, honey," Mitch said hurriedly, "we just got a tip that the suspect we've been looking for in a molestation case has been sighted down in Imperial Beach. The slippery son of a bitch has run out of luck. And I gotta go. Love you."

Coward that she was, she was relieved.

She changed into shorts and a T-shirt, then curled up on the futon with Laura's journal. It was eerie, reading the day-to-day musings during the last seven months of a young woman's life, but even so, Sydney couldn't keep her eyes open past February . . .

Twenty

The ringing phone intruded on her dreams.

A little disoriented at being woken from a sound sleep, Sydney sat up and ran a hand through her hair, pushing it out of her face. The shadows in the room suggested it was near dusk, and she reached to turn on a lamp before grabbing the phone.

"May I speak to Sydney Bryant?" a female voice asked hesitantly.

"This is she."

"Ms. Bryant, this is Tiki Everly."

At last, she thought.

"I'm sorry I missed you this afternoon; I understand you want to talk to me about Laura Clifford."

"Absolutely," Sydney said, noting the use of Laura's maiden name. "As soon as possible. Tonight, tomorrow, you name it."

"Oh . . . well, I'd hate to drag you out on a Saturday night."

"Tonight is fine with me," she said, all at once anxious to get on with it.

"If you're sure it's no bother, perhaps around eight o'clock?"

Sydney glanced at her watch; it was a few minutes past seven. "Perfect. I'll see you then." As she started to hang up, she heard Tiki say something, and brought the phone back to her ear. "Excuse me?"

"I said be careful, Ms. Bryant. Someone's been watching you for several days now."

Startled, she frowned. "What?"

"He's trying to decide if you're a threat to him or not. He could be dangerous."

"Who is he?"

"That isn't clear. But he's watching . . ."

In spite of the fact that she'd never believed in clairvoyance or precognition, Sydney felt a shiver run down her spine.

After changing into her jeans and eating half of a peanut butter sandwich and an apple, she locked up the condo—with more care than usual—and headed back across town, keeping a wary eye on the rearview mirror. Considering the hour and the heavy traffic of Hot August Nights celebrants, though, she couldn't tell if anyone was following her.

She'd been trained in surveillance and tailing techniques while at Dunn Security & Investigations—where the motto was "Consider it Dunn"—and she knew most of the tricks of the trade. Even so, it was surprisingly difficult to spot even a clumsy tail at twilight.

When she made the turn off of 5th Street, however, she did notice a dark-colored mini-van that seemed to gain speed as it passed by. That kind of No-I'm-not-following-you, Look-I'm-driving-right-by stunt was a common mistake for an inexperienced tracker to make.

After pulling into Tiki Everly's driveway, she shut off the engine and killed the lights, then waited in the car for a couple of minutes to see if the van would circle back and cruise the street. It did not.

"So much for paranoia," she said, determined not to obsess about a threat she wasn't sure was real.

Tiki Everly was everything Douglas Foster had claimed her to be—and more. Dressed in a black and gold silk robe, her frizzy hair died an improbable shade of red, she looked like a refugee from a fly-by-night carnival show. She wore at least thirty thin metal bracelets on each wrist, huge garish rings on every finger, and sported five earrings on each ear. For good measure, her nose was pierced with a diamond stud, as was her right eyebrow.

And there was a tattoo along her neck, a thin green stem that blossomed into a small blood red rose in front of her left ear.

Presumably the rose and facial piercings were fairly recent manifestations of Tiki's right to express herself. Sydney could not imagine Douglas Foster omitting either detail from his description of this "exotic creature."

Physically, Tiki was petite and waif-like. Her skin was pale almost to the point of transparency, and she had pretty, cool green eyes.

Sydney introduced herself, displaying her California Investigator's license.

"No need for that," Tiki said, holding the screen door open for her. "I can tell you are who you say you are. Did you see anyone?"

"You mean, was I followed?"

"Yes."

"I'm not sure."

Tiki stepped out on the porch, tilted her head back, closed her eyes, and stood motionless. After a moment, she shook her head, her earrings jangling. "He isn't near. Not now."

Sydney refrained from comment, her attention drawn to

the striking decor of the front room. The walls were painted a dark, midnight blue and adorned with a galaxy of gold and silver stars, like those used by teachers to mark excellent behavior on the citizenship chart back in her elementary school days.

There were planets as well—she recognized Jupiter by its giant red spot and Saturn by its glorious collection of rings—along with other astronomical entities like comets and meteors. The moon, in all its phases, traced an orbit along the far wall.

The place was sparsely furnished, with a black-draped round table holding court in the center of the room, attended by half a dozen high-backed wood chairs. On the table sat a crystal ball on a black Lucite base.

The pungent scent of incense hung thick in the still air; there did not appear to be any windows to provide for ventilation.

Recessed fixtures in the ceiling provided spot lighting, with blue-colored low-watt bulbs. The effect was mystical . . . and somewhat disconcerting.

"This is my reading room. Nice, isn't it?" Tiki asked, closing and locking the front door. "I did it all by myself, from the Khahoutek comet, to the Perseid meteor shower, to the last star in the Little Dipper."

"It is amazing," Sydney agreed.

"Why don't we talk in the back? I made fresh lemonade, and Hortensia baked some double-fudge brownies. With icing, bless her heart."

Sydney followed her down a narrow hallway, at the same time noticing that Ms. Everly was barefoot, as she reportedly had been at the wedding fifteen years ago. There were silver rings on each of her little toes that tapped softly as she walked on the hardwood floor.

Considering the eclectic setting of the reading room, Sydney wasn't sure what to expect in the remainder of the house, but the pale yellow and peach kitchen was entirely normal, with a charming breakfast nook set in a deep bay window, and a walk-in pantry.

On the table was a Blue Willow platter stacked with brownies. Pale blue linen napkins filled a small wicker basket, next to a cut-glass vase of fresh pink, white, and blue carnations.

"Have a seat," Tiki said, going to the refrigerator for the lemonade, "and a brownie. My godmother is the best cook I know."

"Where is Hortensia, by the way?" Sydney asked.

"Out bopping. She put on her poodle skirt and saddle shoes and walked downtown to Ruby's Diner to see Lil' Elmo and the Cosmos." Tiki poured lemonade into tall fountain glasses. "She's a big fan of rock'n'roll; she went to see Sha Na Na on Thursday, and Paul Revere and the Raiders last night."

"Sounds like fun."

"*This* is fun," Tiki said as she brought the glasses to the table and sat down opposite Sydney. She reached for a brownie, took a bite, and moaned. "There are day's I'd kill for chocolate."

"Speaking of which . . ."

"Oh!" Tiki's expression turned serious. "I'm sorry. What an awful thing for me to say. Here I am, a *sensitive*, and what comes out of my mouth but trash."

"Don't worry, I know what you meant."

"It's not that simple. There's a cosmic price to be paid for cluttering up the human consciousness with violent words. Take a look around at all the trouble in the world. The bill is coming due."

Uncertain how to respond to that, she opted not to. "I need to talk to you about Laura."

"Yes, I know." Tiki put the half-eaten brownie on one of the napkins and delicately licked the frosting from her fingers. "I've been waiting for you."

"For me specifically?"

"Well, I didn't know your name, but I knew there would be someone looking into Laura's murder this summer. You're going to catch him."

"That's reassuring."

"I mean it." Tiki reached across the table and touched Sydney lightly on the back on the hand. "You're already closer than you think."

Which wasn't saying much, Sydney thought ruefully. She couldn't remember a case where she'd felt less sure of where or to whom the evidence was leading. If this were a multiple-choice exam, she'd have to pick "None of the Above" as her answer.

Aware that Tiki was waiting expectantly, she said, "I hope you're right."

"Oh, I am."

"In the meantime, why don't you tell me about your friendship with Laura. How long had you known her?"

"About four years. We met in the summer of 1981, when I was fifteen."

"Here in Reno?"

Tiki nodded. "At the rodeo, believe it or not. Laura was nineteen, I think, and she was dating a cowboy she'd met down in Texas. She followed him to Reno, only after she got here, she decided that maybe the rodeo circuit wasn't all she'd bargained for."

"But Reno was?"

"She liked the lifestyle. Bright lights, little city, open

twenty-four hours a day. And she got a lot of attention from men who weren't always having to scrape the horse shit off their boots."

Sydney laughed. "I can see the attraction."

"Anyway, we met in the concession line, buying popcorn, got to talking, and hit it off." Tiki frowned. "What's sad is I knew from the start that Laura would come to a tragic end."

Sydney felt the hair rise on the nape of her neck. "Did you warn her?"

"Many times. Like a lot of people, she wanted to believe only the good things I saw in her future. She would never listen to the bad."

"What exactly did you see happening?"

"That Laura would die at an early age. Violently. I saw a lot of blood."

"And how is it you saw this?"

"I can't explain it, really." Tiki twirled a strand of hair between her index and middle fingers. "I get, I guess you'd call them *images,* in my mind."

"Like a movie?"

"Sort of, only the focus isn't always great. I can usually tell whose future I'm seeing, but the background is often hazy, the way you'd see something through a fog."

"And this just comes to you?"

"Most of the time, yes. Now and then I have to work at it, concentrate on opening my mind to let it in."

Sydney frowned, troubled by the notion of life being predestined, of hurtling unknowingly towards a fixed future that couldn't be changed . . .

Tiki took a sip of lemonade and made a face. "This could use a little sweetening," she said and got up, crossing to a cupboard. She returned with a lidded bowl and measured a generous tablespoon of brown granulated sugar into her glass, where it settled to the bottom, along with a few stray lemon seeds. "Want some?"

Although she had yet to taste it, she slid the glass across the table. "Do you get images for everyone you pass on the street?"

"No, thank God." Tiki spooned sugar into Sydney's glass and gave it a quick stir. "I'd be in Intensive Care if I did. Too much can be overwhelming, totally exhausting. It makes me dizzy. Have you ever had labyrinthitis? It's like that, feels like the room is spinning. I've even thrown up a few times. No, there has to be contact."

"Physical contact?"

"Most of the time, but if I handle an object that belongs to a person, I can usually connect with them. For example, you gave Hortensia your card, and you'd written your phone number on the back. That was all I needed to tap in."

"How long have you had this gift?"

"As long as I can remember. It gets stronger every year, though, so I'm *much* better at it now than I was way back when."

"Are you ever wrong?"

Tiki sighed. "Not that I know of. Of course, I don't always hear how things turn out. People tend to freak when you tell them the dark stuff."

"The dark stuff," Sydney echoed. "Meaning how they're going to die?"

"Among other things. It's true what they say about there being a fate worse than death . . . but I'd rather not talk about that."

"Fine with me."

"Anyway, as I said, I warned Laura, but only in a general way. I couldn't give her a date or a place or a time."

"Or who?"

"Unfortunately, no. I might have been able to if I'd touched him that day—"

"You're certain it's a man?"

"That much I *do* know."

"Did you dance with any of the male guests at the reception?" she asked, thinking she could reduce the suspect list by process of elimination.

"I only had the energy for one dance. I wasn't feeling well that day, probably because I was picking up the death vibrations and didn't know it. Anyway, it was with Brad, and you already know he didn't do it."

Sydney didn't ask how *she* knew that. "That would leave three possible suspects, if in fact the killer attended the reception."

"He followed them into the desert."

"So it has to be Alan Foster, Randy Leighton, or Gary West."

"Hmm. Well, technically, yes."

"Technically?"

"Don't forget the photographer."

"What?"

"The guy who took the wedding pictures. He was there for the cutting of the cake and all of that."

"No one mentioned a photographer," Sydney said, shaking her head at the countless items of information that hadn't made it into the police files or witness statements.

"Really? I thought Mr. Foster would have, but maybe not. Rich people don't always notice their hirelings. And the photographer wasn't there for very long. Less than an hour, I'd say."

"Even so—"

"But it couldn't be him," Tiki said, "if you weren't aware of him until now. The feeling I'm getting from the man who's watching you is that he's worried you're closing in."

"Nevertheless, I'd like to talk to the photographer. And I'd be very interested in having a look at the wedding pictures."

"I would too. I might be able to pick up something . . . I know of other sensitives who have the ability to read from photographs . . . at least I could try."

"I don't suppose you recall a name?"

Tiki shook her head. "I never knew his name. He was an older man, kind of abrupt, even rude. The only thing he said to me was 'smile.' But Mr. Foster should know, or least be able to find out."

"Right. Back to the other three . . . I understand that you've seen or talked to Randy on occasion here in town."

"Yes."

"Is he the one?"

"I don't think so, but . . ."

"Don't you know?"

"I'm not psychic. Understand that I can't reach out with my mind and *sample* people's thoughts like I'm at a smorgasbord. I can only receive whatever's being sent, after the initial mental link has been made." Tiki leaned forward, bracelets clunking on the table where she rested her arms. "It's a little complicated, but *time* also affects the signal. Time, distance, and the person's state of mind. So do drugs or alcohol."

"Meaning?"

"Meaning if Randy had done it, but wasn't feeling any anxiety about it or was intoxicated, I wouldn't necessarily get anything from him."

"I see," Sydney said, although she didn't. It seemed to her that no matter how many years had passed, the killer should feel a persistent and pervasive sense of distress at having brutally slaughtered two human beings. "But whoever killed them *is* anxious now, right?"

"Very."

"Then if you confronted him now, you'd know?" Not that a sensitive's perceptions would ever qualify as evidence in any court of law.

"I think so . . ." Her voice trailed off and she touched her head somewhat gingerly.

"What is it?"

Tiki's green eyes widened. "I think he's . . ." She hesitated and stood, swaying slightly.

"Are you okay?"

"Oh," Tiki said. She took a step, her eyes rolled back, and she slumped to the floor in a dead faint.

Twenty-One

"Are you sure you're all right?"

Tiki Everly smiled wanly, but her voice was remarkably steady. "I'm fine. I guess so much of my consciousness was focused *outward,* there wasn't enough here to keep me, well, *here.*"

"It's happened before?"

"Many times. Like letting go of the string, and watching the balloon float away. It's a very peaceful feeling, actually."

"As long as the balloon comes back."

"Ah, but you can get another balloon," Tiki said serenely.

Which was a little too metaphysical for her taste. "There is one other thing . . . in Laura's journal, she refers to having 'black dreams' and mentions that she hadn't told Sean about what you said about them."

"Wow . . . it's *such* a bad idea to write about the dreams!"

"How is that?"

"Writing about them kind of gives them form. Makes them real. I wouldn't do it, that's for sure."

"What were the dreams about?"

"The other world." Tiki hugged herself, rubbing her arms as though to warm them. "Where people go who die brutally . . . the way she did."

"And what did you say that she couldn't or wouldn't tell Sean?"

"That he was at risk, too. She'd been having dreams about her own death, that she was being chased and killed. Then a week or so before the wedding, she dreamed that Sean was there . . . and someone shot him in the head."

Startled, Sydney frowned. "What?"

"People foretell their own deaths more often than you might imagine," Tiki said. "Not as clearly or in as much detail as that, but you'd be surprised. Unless they tell someone, though, nobody is ever aware of it. Add all the people who claim never to remember their dreams, and it's not uncommon."

"I'm not sure I'd want to know."

Tiki shrugged. "Not everyone has a choice."

"Don't forget to call," Tiki said as they stood at the front door, "if you want me to have a go at the wedding pictures."

"I will."

Sydney watched her rearview mirror for several blocks until she was satisfied that no one was following her. Driving with the windows down, she savored the balmy summer night. Above, the sky was sprinkled with stars, the moon partially hidden behind a wisp of cloud. The storm Hortensia had predicted was off in the distance to the east, complete with flashes of lightning and the faint rumble of thunder.

Sometime after midnight, the moon would disappear behind the ridge of mountains, the clouds would dissipate, and the night would turn velvet black.

In the desert, away from the neon glare of city lights, the dark would be absolute and total. Somewhere in that darkness, the mortal remains of Sean Foster were scattered like a child's pick-up sticks, waiting to be stumbled upon by the next hapless hiker.

Until then, he was alone out there. The thought haunted her.

It was nearly ten-thirty when she arrived at the condo—traffic on Virginia Street had been diverted as exuberant cruisers honked and hooted their way through downtown Reno—but despite the late hour, she went straight to the kitchen phone and dialed Douglas Foster's number.

The phone rang seven times before Martha Barclay answered. "Foster residence."

"This is Sydney Bryant," she said. "I'm sorry for calling at this hour, but I need to talk to Mr. Foster."

"Of course, only can I have him call you back? He's only just gotten into the pool for his evening swim."

"That's fine. I'll be up till late. Tell him, would you, that I'm interested in seeing the photographs of the wedding and reception, and it is urgent—"

"Shall I interrupt his therapy?"

"That isn't necessary, although I do need a call back tonight, and I also need the name and phone number of the photographer."

"I'll tell him as soon as he comes up for air," the housekeeper promised.

In the living room, she saw the message light blinking on the answering machine, and a fax in the tray. She checked the fax and found a typed information sheet on Tiki from her office, giving a current address and listing her memberships—in good standing—in the Society of Alternative Consciousness, the Northern Nevada Sensitives' Alliance, the Sierra Chapter of Mystics, and the American Association of Alien Abductees, besides which Hannah had written "UFO group, based in Rachel, Nevada."

Sydney shook her head. If it were to come to that, she could imagine a defense attorney's glee at the prospect of going to court with Tiki Everly as a star prosecution witness. A few salient questions about her professional affiliations and beliefs, and the jury would be in stitches.

She hit Play and turned up the volume on the answering machine.

"Sydney, honey, it's your mother. It's Saturday here . . . what am I saying? It must be Saturday there, too, unless they've moved the International Dateline. Whatever. I talked to Ethan this morning, and I hope you're not upset with me. I'm only trying to help, sweetheart. You know that, don't you dear? Call me."

There was a second or two of silence followed by a dial tone and a beep.

"Hey, it's me," Xavier said. "Since I'm talking to a machine, you must be out working. The reason I'm calling is to tell you that I'll be free to fly up to Reno by Monday evening, or Tuesday morning at the latest. I did my gig testifying—and knocked it out of the ballpark if I do say so myself—but the judge told me to hang tight over the weekend, because there might be redirect on Monday, yadda, yadda, yadda. Anyway, reinforcements are on the way, partner. *Ciao.*"

Another beep. The third call was a slow hang-up, in that she could hear whoever it was fumbling with the phone before the line went dead. And in the background, ever so faintly but eerily apropos, she heard the Coasters' classic song, "Searchin'."

The next message was from Tiki Everly, who apparently had called while she was en route home.

"All the talk about dreams reminded me of a recurring dream I've had about Laura's keys. I don't know what the significance is, but I remember she had a brass key ring, because she took off her wedding band—the heat made her fingers puffy and it was too tight—and slipped it onto the key ring for safekeeping. Anyway—"

Sydney reached over quickly to replay the last part of the message.

"—because she took off her wedding band—the heat made her fingers puffy and it was too tight—and slipped it onto the key ring for safekeeping. Anyway, I've had these dreams and I thought you should know. That key ring might be a link to Laura."

She let the tape run as she got up to find her copy of the police report listing the personal effects recovered at the crime scene. The tape hissed softly; there were no further messages.

Indeed, when she located the report, there was no mention of keys in the inventory of Laura's purse. Besides a wallet containing $23.75 in cash and a checkbook with a recorded balance of $317.99, the purse held only a "yellow metal" compact and a lipstick.

She thumbed through the reports to the vehicle inventory, on the chance that Laura's keys had been left on the seat with the bridal bouquet Xavier had described seeing, or perhaps had fallen to the floor, but again, there was no key ring listed.

Maybe Sean had been using her keys. It was entirely possible that in the rush to leave, he had lost or misplaced his and borrowed hers. But would she even have had keys to his car?

"Shit." She'd gotten a totally unexpected answer as to the burning question of what had happened to the bride's wedding band, only to have an equally perplexing question arise in its stead. In theory, at least, a key ring should be easier to find, if only because it was a slightly larger needle in the haystack.

★ ★ ★ ★ ★

At twenty after eleven, the phone finally rang.

"Ms. Bryant," Douglas Foster said, his manner formal. "Martha tells me you're inquiring after the wedding photos. May I ask why?"

Foster was not the kind of a man who'd be comfortable with an unorthodox method of investigation, but as her client he was entitled to an explanation . . . of a sort. "I can't go into any detail, unfortunately, but I've developed a source of information in the case."

"What source?"

"I'm not at liberty to say, but I've reached a critical stage of the investigation, and I need to be as thorough as possible."

"Just a moment," Foster said abruptly.

Sydney heard a muffled exchange as Foster apparently covered the phone with his hand. She waited, wondering what the odds were that she would be able to interview the photographer tomorrow.

"I apologize for the interruption, but Alan just reminded me that I, that is, *we*, never got the wedding album from the photographer."

"Why not?"

"In the beginning, it was too painful to even consider looking at the pictures. Time passed, but regrettably, it must have slipped my mind. I can give you the name of the photographer, however—it must be in my records somewhere—and I will certainly call him in the morning to give him permission to release the album to you."

"That'll work." She hesitated. "Did you say that Alan is there?"

"Yes, he's here, why do you ask?"

The truth was a little awkward, since she had in fact considered Alan a suspect in his brother's death—something Douglas Foster might not appreciate—but if Alan's whereabouts could be accounted for throughout the evening, he could not have been the person who Tiki sensed was following her. She punted as best she could, saying, "I had a question for him, actually. I tried to call him at home, oh, around eight or eight-thirty, but there was no answer."

"Yes, well, he and Valerie arrived at six."

And then there were two, she thought.

"Do you want to talk to him?"

"No, no. It can wait till tomorrow."

"Are you sure? He's standing right here."

Having backed herself into a corner, she had no choice. "All right, sure, if it's no bother."

"No bother at all," the elder Foster assured her.

"Ms. Bryant, good evening." Alan came on the line, his tone distinctly upbeat compared to this morning's interview. "You have a question for me?"

"Yes." Naturally, her mind went blank and the only thing she could think of on short notice was Laura's key ring—and what its disappearance might signify. "What kind of a car did Laura drive?"

"She had two cars, oddly enough, for as little money as she made, although both were kind of old and beat up. Most of the time she drove a red, two-door Toyota, but she also had a Subaru Brat."

"That's a four-wheel drive?"

"The Brat is, yes."

Was it possible that the killer had used Laura's car in the commission of the murders?

"—is late," Alan Foster was saying, "if there's nothing else."

"That's all, except . . . do you know if anyone ever found

Laura's keys? They were missing from her purse."

"I hadn't heard. Maybe she gave them to a friend so they could water her plants."

Or someone who wasn't a friend took the keys so he could use her car without anyone knowing. Or suspecting.

Twenty-Two

Sunday

When the sun rose at 6:02 A.M., Sydney had already been up for an hour. Using her laptop, she'd accessed the computer server at her office and spent about twenty minutes entering addresses into a nifty little mapping program which calculated mileage between given sites. She had copied the addresses of Erin Cross, Gary West, Brad Goldwyn, and Tiki Everly from their 1985 police statements. For the sake of thoroughness, she also included Alan's office address.

And she'd found Laura's address on a photocopy of the dead woman's driver's license that had been tucked among Xavier's case notes. She had the office computer crunch the numbers, then directed it to fax a hard copy to her in Reno on a two-minute delay.

She unplugged the laptop, plugged the fax back into the telephone jack, and went to the kitchen for a Pepsi while she waited.

A few minutes later, armed with her data, a city map, a notepad, and the time-line which she'd finally finished after midnight last night, she hit the road, heading first toward the exclusive neighborhood where Douglas Foster lived.

This early on a Sunday morning, there wasn't a guard on duty; the residents had to enter an access code on a keypad to activate the gates. Evidently, visitors who didn't know the

213

code were plum out of luck until a guard arrived to check the approved guest list and let them in.

It wasn't her intention to call on anyone, so she made a U-turn in the "reject lane" in front of the guard complex—provided so those unfortunates deemed unworthy of entrance could be sent on their way without inconveniencing the chosen few by obstructing traffic—and backed up to the wrought-iron gate.

From this common starting point, she meant to derive a rough estimate of how much time it might have taken each witness and/or suspect to drive from Point A—the Foster residence—to Point B—their homes or in Alan's case, his office—and ultimately to Point C—the murder site.

Still, she was well aware of the fact that she could only approximate the road and traffic conditions of fifteen years past, but at least she'd have reasonably accurate information on which to base her conclusions. And getting the lay of the land might help clarify her thinking, adding another piece to the puzzle that was just beginning to take shape in her mind.

Erin Cross had lived nearest to the Fosters, on a tree-lined street in what was now and almost certainly had been then a quiet neighborhood of single-family homes and duplexes. The yards were big and well tended, the houses small but solidly constructed, the prevailing architectural style a stucco bungalow.

Sydney pulled to the curb in front of a pastel-pink duplex at 425 Marigold. Erin Cross had rented the B-unit, to the back of the lot. It was here, Ms. Cross claimed, she had come after leaving the reception at four-thirty.

Sydney made note that it had taken twelve minutes to get here from the house on the hill. Plenty of time.

Although she was inclined to agree with Tiki that it had

been a man who'd killed Laura and Sean, she dared not risk developing her own "confirmation bias," looking only for facts that fit her suspicions. She could not ignore the possibility that despite her protestations, Erin was indeed a woman scorned.

By her own account, on the day of the murders Erin Cross had been living alone, her family hundreds of miles away in Las Vegas. She wasn't dating, in part due to the pressures and demands of law school, and yet she'd found time in her hectic schedule to catch the act of her ex-boyfriend's pretty bride-to-be.

Had it been simple curiosity or latent jealousy?

Whichever, she was subsequently humiliated to find herself an uninvited guest at the wedding. She could see that Douglas Foster was annoyed and imagined his irritation was directed at her. If that wasn't unpleasant enough, Sean had taken the opportunity to run off at the mouth about how happy he was, having found true love for the first time in his life, in effect dismissing their own long-term romantic involvement, maliciously or not.

For good measure, she'd watched Sean and his handsome young cousin nearly come to blows over a woman she obviously considered to be a gold-digger and a tramp.

Had her hurt and resentment turned to hatred and a desire to kill?

Sydney had to admit that theory was somewhat consistent with the manner of death of the victims. Laura's murder was viciously brutal—there was little doubt she was the true target of the killer's rage—while Sean had apparently been dispatched almost mercifully with a single bullet to the head.

Erin remained a possibility, all else aside.

Next in order was the apartment building on Dove Street, where Gary West had dreamed of Porsches and high concepts, waiting to get rich quick. It was a mile and seven-tenths from Erin's place, no more than two or three minutes away.

There were perhaps thirty apartments divided between three two-story buildings that enclosed the dirt courtyard on three sides. A child's wading pool sat in the shade of a liquid amber tree, maybe six feet from a redwood picnic table on which stood a small battalion of empty beer cans, the prover-bial dead soldiers of drinking lore.

Gary had lived in #11 with an unnamed roommate who reportedly was in Oakland at an A's double-header on the day in question. That and West's rather lame casino-hopping alibi provided opportunity.

Motive was a little iffy. There had clearly been no love lost between the best man and the bride, but despite that, as far as she knew there hadn't been a specific incident that would trigger a killing. And would he have shot his friend and future business partner? That was problematic, in particular since Sean seemed to be willing and financially able to bankroll the health spa if their business loan fell through.

Foolish to slay the goose that laid the golden egg.

Although . . . Laura had been concerned enough about their joint venture to consult Alan about it, possibly even be-hind Sean's back. What if Gary had gotten wind of that? Would it be enough to provoke him to commit murder?

Maybe.

He, too, would fit the profile of a killer whose fury had been directed primarily at Laura.

Laura's apartment was third on her list, and after con-sulting the map to verify the directions, she headed that way. It was just after 7 A.M., and the streets were still deserted. There were, however, a bevy of stop signs en route to the Virginia Lake area, and it took twenty-one minutes to reach the address on Goldleaf Lane.

At her prior stops she had remained in the car, content to see what she could from the street. Here, she cut the engine and got out for a closer look.

This was a small complex, eight units on one level, bracketing an in-ground pool. There was a gate here, too, but this one stood open, welcoming rather than forbidding. There was no one in sight.

Sydney followed the red faded cement walk to #6, stopping for a moment in front of the door, inexplicably tempted to knock. There was something other-worldly about the pale morning light and the whisper of wind that made her wonder . . . if she knocked, would Laura answer?

"You're working too hard," she said under her breath, but she remained where she was, her attention riveted to the door.

From this apartment, Laura Clifford had left to begin her married life. On that Saturday morning in August 1985, the future must have seemed bright, full of promise and endless possibilities.

What had she been thinking as she walked out that door? Was she happy? Nervous? Or perhaps simply overwhelmed at the prospect of joining her fate to Sean's? Maybe there'd even been a touch of sadness at leaving all that was familiar to her behind.

Whichever, it was not to be.

To have met her death so suddenly and savagely, within hours of what presumably had been the most joyous moment in her young life, seemed cruel beyond measure. The very cold-bloodedness of the act compelled Sydney to persist in the search for the truth and a final resolution in this case, long overdue.

After one last look, she turned and walked away.

Brad Goldwyn's former apartment was only a few blocks away, and even though he had what she considered to be a pretty solid alibi, she wasn't leaving any stone unturned. If only to get everything straight in her head, she wanted to see the place.

But there wasn't anything *to* see; the apartments had been razed, making way for a small professional building on the corner lot.

She thought about a little boy laughing at ducks and eating Spaghetti-Os, and the relentless passage of time.

Alan Foster's office at Musique Recording, Ltd. was located in an industrial area near the airport on Matley Lane. From what she could tell by looking through the glass door, the office itself was nondescript; there was a small reception area into which was crowded a secretary's desk and chair, two velvet wing chairs, a leather couch, and a coffee table scattered with *Rolling Stone* magazines, *Daily Variety*, and sheet music.

The walls were covered with framed photographs of what she gathered was the firm's clientele, running the gamut from spiky-haired rock artists to down-home country performers and a polka band. There were also several old vinyl records that appeared to have been nailed to the wall, and a life-size poster of the Rocket Man, Elton John, wearing a pair of his trademark space cadet glasses.

To the left was a padded door marked Studio, with a light-box above it that read "In Session." On the right, a second door had Alan Foster's name painted on the frosted glass insert in black script, the word "President" directly below. According to Alan, he'd sought refuge from the world behind that door on the evening his brother and former lover were murdered.

Last night, she had been inclined to dismiss him as a suspect, since his uncle had voluntarily supplied him with an alibi for the time period when she was supposedly being followed. But it occurred to her that of the original six potential suspects, he really was the only one with the financial wherewithal to have *paid* someone to do his dirty work, either the murders or the intimidation tactics.

In any case, Sydney supposed that he, too, might have been angrier at Laura for betraying him than he was at Sean, his own flesh and blood. It never ceased to amaze her how often men in these triangles chose to direct the greater part of their hostility at the woman, rather than the other man. Might he have come to view her as a seductress who'd led Sean astray?

The stabbing itself could even be viewed from the perspective of a wronged male, seeking to destroy a cheating heart.

Perhaps Alan had shown mercy to Sean, comparatively speaking, as a consequence of their shared upbringing, a relic of the "us against the world" mind-set of a conscientious older brother.

Which meant that she could not eliminate him from suspicion yet.

In 1985, Tiki Everly had lived in Shady Oaks, a trailer park south of town.

True to its name, the park was amply shaded by a grove of mature oak trees. The trailers were of the travel variety—with names like Nomad, Rambler, Vacationeer, and Prowler—intended to be towed behind a car. There were a few newer models, but the majority had some hard miles on them, visible in dings and dents, in rusting fenders and weathered siding.

A fair number of these wheeled residences had been thoroughly domesticated, complete with flower boxes, frilly curtains, screen doors, canopies, clotheslines, and TV antennas, but a few had resisted grounding and looked as if all that held them here was a power cord.

Sydney drove slowly along the gravel road that wound its way through the park, taking notice of a small laundry room and a playground with a sandbox and a jungle gym. The park manager was located to the rear of the property, in a single-width mobile home with an enclosed porch.

It was now 8:45 A.M., but the only resident she saw was a tabby cat that walked across the road in front of her, tail high in the air.

Still, she had a sense that her slow progress was being monitored from behind curtains and just inside screen doors. She doubted there were many visitors to the park, and she imagined the people who lived there—by choice or necessity—were as suspicious of strangers as the desert rats Jim Wagner had described.

She had no intention of disturbing anyone on a Sunday morning and drove on slowly, her mind toying with the notion of Tiki Everly as a suspect. Toying because of how unlikely that seemed, in that the fortune teller claimed to have never learned to drive, and to a lesser degree because of her diminutive size.

As for the question of motive, there was none apparent. Tiki seemed genuinely fond of Laura, and alone among the guests had actually made it through the reception without causing or participating in any kind of scene. Nor did she appear to have had a romantic or financial interest in either the bride or the groom.

But in her line of work, even the least likely suspect deserved consideration. There was always a chance that everything that Ms. Everly had told her was so much hokum, designed to distract her or convince her not to take a hard look.

Arriving again at the front of the park, Sydney braked to a stop near a long row of battered mailboxes. She glanced in the rearview mirror and was able to make out the dark shape of a man standing in the doorway of a Traveleze, three trailers back. "Must be from the Welcome Wagon," she said to his hulking silhouette.

She gave the Probe enough gas to spin the tires and spit gravel as she turned left onto the road. A little attitude once in awhile never hurt.

At 9:25 A.M., she returned to the guard gate. There was now a guard on duty, and she passed by the private entrance to make a U-turn further down the road. As she drove by the entrance a second time, she considered Randy Leighton and his bike.

The fact was Leighton had placed high on the suspect list. His motorcycle gave him the means, and his altercation with Sean gave him a motive. His lack of an alibi—although clearly the norm in this case—did not exonerate him, no matter how wishful his thinking.

His youth was another consideration; at seventeen, he would arguably have been more impulsive than an adult. His self-described "constant state of arousal" could conceivably be symptomatic of something more complex than a teenager's raging hormones; although she wasn't an expert in psychology, she'd read enough to know that there was a school of thought which connected a hyperactive sex drive with an anger control disorder.

It was certainly within the realm of possibility that Randy had misinterpreted Laura's interest in him. Their provocative dance, the near-fight, and the hateful words could easily have gotten his blood up. And despite what he'd said about not being bothered over the disparity in his cousin's financial circumstances and his own, there might have been a lingering undercurrent of resentment to add fuel to the fire.

Perhaps he had followed them into the desert, watching as the car broke down, then hanging back until Sean was out of sight. Or maybe he'd given Sean a ride, offering to take him for help. That made perfect sense, and would explain why Laura had stayed behind.

Had he driven his cousin off-road with the intent to shoot him?

Had he made advances to Laura afterwards, only to be rebuffed? If she had laughed at him or belittled him, would that have triggered a killing rage? It was at least possible.

Lost in thought, Sydney missed her turn and had to circle the block. Traffic—which had been all but nonexistent until nine—was backed up as drivers slowed to admire a silver 1941 Willys which was parked, hood up, on the side of the road.

"What kind of engine is that?" she heard someone ask as she inched by.

"It's a 454, supercharged." The proud owner beamed. "This baby can go from zero to 160 miles an hour in a quarter mile and 9.65 seconds."

"Awesome!"

She shook her head, unable to fathom the male need for speed. It reminded her, too, of Randy Leighton's admission that he had once driven from Reno to Austin in a little over two hours. She wondered if his personal best had been recorded on that hot August night.

There was a message from Douglas Foster on the answering machine when she arrived at the condo, a few minutes before ten o'clock.

"It seems," he said, "that the photographer who took the wedding pictures died several years ago, but I managed to reach his sister, who told me she's kept most of his equipment and files. She wasn't sure whether the photos are among them, but she did say you're more than welcome to have a look."

"Great," Sydney murmured as she sat down and turned up the volume.

"And I've authorized her to release any photographs or negatives directly to you," Foster added. "I'm not sure yet if I want to see them myself, but . . . never mind. Anyway, her name is Sally Davenport, she lives down in Washoe Valley, and she's expecting your call."

Flipping to a blank page in her notebook, she wrote down the number as he recited it.

Foster cleared his throat. "I'm not sure what your schedule is like, but since Miss Davenport was nice enough to agree to see you on a Sunday, I would suggest that you make an effort to do so."

"Yes, Sir," she said, saluting the machine.

"And call me when you've—"

The machine beeped, signaling that it had cut him off in mid-sentence.

Such was life, she thought, reaching for the phone.

Twenty-Three

"Found your way, did you?" Sally Davenport said, stepping out on her porch as Sydney started up the stairs. She looked to be in her early fifties, a tall, raw-boned woman with a graying ponytail, dressed in jeans, work boots, and a man's blue denim shirt worn open over a white T-shirt. "Not everyone does; folks tell me I give lousy directions."

"I've had a little practice lately at reading maps," Sydney said matter-of-factly. "Thank you for making time for this."

The woman shrugged. "There's not much else to do on a Sunday after church. Come on in and I'll show you Richard's stuff."

Sydney followed her through an immaculate house, decorated in Early American, down a hallway that made a sharp left turn to what appeared to be a dead end. Sally Davenport reached up to the low ceiling, grabbed an ornate metal ring, and pulled down a folding staircase.

"It gets a little warm up in the attic come summertime, but there's a fan up there that'll at least move the hot air around."

"No problem."

"If it gets too stifling, feel free to help yourself to an iced tea or a soda in the kitchen. I'll be in the garden out back if you need me."

"Thanks." Sydney peered up into the attic as she tested the first step.

224

"You know," Ms. Davenport said, pausing as she headed down the hall, "I almost threw my brother's junk out during spring cleaning. I held onto it for sentimental reasons, but he died in 1994 and this is the only time anyone's ever shown an interest in any of it. But I hope you find what you're looking for."

"So do I," she said, even though she wasn't exactly sure what that might be.

Sydney found a switch to the right of the stairs and turned on the light, a bare hundred-watt bulb that hung down from the wood rafters. The fan had been installed in the attic vent, and she went over to turn that on, given the heat and the stagnant air.

Richard Davenport's "junk" was in four, two-drawer gray metal file cabinets that were lined up in a neat row at the gable end of the attic. The cabinet drawers were unlabeled, and when she opened the first, she saw why: perhaps hundreds of 9" x 12" manila envelopes had been simply dumped inside, with no attempt at organization.

"Oh boy," she said as she selected an envelope from the top of the pile. It too was unlabeled and had never been sealed. She opened the flap and brought out a jumble of photo proofs of what appeared to be a little girl's birthday party, compete with party favors, balloon animals, and a maniacal-looking clown.

She spotted a small white envelope among the proofs and plucked it out. It contained the negatives and an index card that gave the subject's name, address, and phone number, as well as the date the photographs were taken. There were also other notations that she assumed referred to the type of film used, the number of shots taken, and the date that the proofs had been reviewed by the customer prior to ordering the final photos.

"And all I have to do is find the Foster-Clifford wedding pictures. Piece of cake."

A trickle of sweat ran down her spine as she grabbed a handful of the envelopes, sat Indian-style on the floor, and began to go through them, one by one.

Even with the fan blowing directly at her, the heat was oppressive, and by the time an hour had passed, her cotton blouse and the waistband of her jeans were soaked through with perspiration. Adding to her discomfort, she kept sneezing from the dust, her hands were filthy from handling the envelopes, she had sustained about a million paper cuts—which stung like mad—and her rear end was sore.

The second hour, after a break for an ice-cold bottle of orange soda, she worked her way through the second file cabinet, kneeling on the floor in front of it. Her hair was wringing wet, clinging stubbornly to her neck. And she had to stop what she was doing every few minutes to wipe her face on a paper towel, so that she didn't sweat all over other peoples' memories.

Midway through the third hour, she got cramps in both legs and had to walk it out, alternately stretching her calf muscles and twisting gently from side to side to ease a kink in her back. She unbuttoned her blouse and stood directly in front of the fan, the air slightly cooling as it dried her damp skin.

Regardless, the moment she saw Laura's face, all else was forgotten.

There were only a few developed proofs in the envelope— presumably because there had been no one to review them— but she estimated there were perhaps forty-some negative strips, each with six photographs, for an approximate total of two hundred fifty pictures. The index card verified that Davenport had used seven rolls of a high quality 35mm Kodak film, with thirty-six exposures per roll.

"Looks like we're in business, boys and girls," she said, smiling in relief.

As anxious as she was to look at them, this wasn't the time or place to do so; besides her reluctance to handle potential evidence in such a dusty environment, the light was inadequate, and it would take a fair amount of time to review the negatives in any detail. And she doubted the suffocating heat was conducive to rational thought.

So, after returning the piles of envelopes back to the cabinets—somewhat more orderly than she had found them—she turned off the fan and the light, and started down the stairs.

Sally Davenport was sitting on the front porch steps, shelling peas. "Find what you were looking for?" she asked without looking up from her chore.

"I did, thank you. Do you want me to sign for these?"

"Oh, there's no need for that. They don't belong to me, and bless his poor occluded heart, Richard has no use for them."

There was no faulting the woman's logic.

It was ten after three before Sydney made it back to Reno. Despite the air conditioning in the car, she felt hot, sticky, and more than a little grimy. Inside the condo, she tossed the manila envelope on the breakfast bar and headed straight upstairs to take a shower.

She stood under the lukewarm water for a very long time, luxuriating in the silky feel of it on her heat-flushed skin. Raising her face to the spray, she closed her eyes and let it pulse against her eyelids.

Only after the water cooled to the point that she began to

shiver did she get out and wrap herself in an over-sized towel. When she could bear it, she slipped into a clean pair of faded jeans and a San Diego Chargers T-shirt, then padded bare-foot downstairs.

The envelope beckoned, and she took it—and a Pepsi—into the living room, searching for adequate light. Removing the shade from the lamp on the end table, she switched it on.

She started by glancing through the photo proofs, all of which were of the bride and groom. Sydney had seen pictures of Sean as a boy and a teenager, but these were the first of him as a young man, at twenty-four. He was good-looking, in a quiet way, dark-haired and dark-eyed, with even features and a winning smile. He was dressed in an expensive-looking and well-tailored navy blue suit, white shirt, and a blue and green striped tie.

For their small, private wedding, Laura had chosen an off-white silk dress that ended just below her knees in a flare. The bodice was delicately embroidered in a floral pattern using pale pink, blue, and gold thread. Her glorious straw-berry blonde hair was gathered coquettishly to one side, where it cascaded over her shoulder, reaching nearly to her waist. Holding her bouquet of tiny pink roses—exactly as Xavier had described—she was the embodiment of a beau-tiful bride.

They made a striking couple.

Sydney propped a photograph of them together against the base of the lamp as yet another reminder of the reason she was here. Then she removed the negative strips from the small envelope, took a deep breath, and held the first of them up to the light.

"Be there," she murmured.

As might be expected, the photographer had started with the traditional posed shots, of Sean and Laura gazing deeply and lovingly into each other's eyes, sharing a rather chaste kiss, and sipping champagne.

They cut the cake and fed each other—Sean did *not* smear cake on his wife's lovely face—and kissed again afterwards. There was a single shot of Laura laughing, while Sean looked perplexed, and then of her oh-so-tenderly wiping the corner of his mouth with a napkin. Laura looked at Sean as if she were delighted by the sight of him.

His expression was somewhat bedazzled, as though he couldn't quite believe his luck at having found her. And in photo after photo, they were touching each other, whether it was her fingertips resting gently on his shoulder or him with a hand on her slender waist or simply their fingers entwined by their sides.

And there was a photograph showing them in each other's arms, preparing to dance, looking at each other with such intensity that you simply knew at that moment, everyone else in the world had ceased to exist. Her chin was tilted up at him, her lips parted invitingly, while his hunger for her was revealed by the possessive way he held her, drinking her in with his eyes.

However cynically others had viewed their relationship, Sydney accepted without reservation that they had been truly and totally in love. Which made what happened to them that much worse . . .

There were also photographs of the bride and groom with Douglas and Alan, as well as each of the guests in turn. These were eminently civilized shots, with everyone on their best behavior, smiling directly into the camera. Among them, only Erin Cross appeared to be ill at ease, forcing a smile.

Still, Sydney assumed that these pictures had been taken *before* the celebration really began. What she hoped was that Davenport had stayed around long enough to catch the members of the wedding party being a little less formal and a lot more real.

And revealing.

She got her wish.

The last ten strips of negatives were candid shots. Seemingly unaware of the photographer's presence, the bride had taken off her heels and was massaging her nyloned foot. In another, she'd bitten into a canapé and made a face like a five-year-old forced to eat liver. And she sat on her new husband's lap and nibbled on his earlobe as he drank from a long-necked beer bottle.

For his part, Sean lost the jacket and tie, unbuttoned his shirt halfway down his chest and rolled up his sleeves. In every single photo, he was either drinking or had a bottle in his hand. In the space of twenty or so photographs, his features began to take on the slackness characteristic of inebriation.

There was a single shot of Erin sitting forlornly by herself, frowning, one hand covering her eyes. She looked miserable, her body language that of someone who wants nothing more than to be gone.

A very young Tiki was in several shots—she was amazingly photogenic in her own quixotic way—most of which showed her hovering near a sumptuous buffet. She was also immortalized licking her fingers, eyes closed in bliss. There was something disarming and even poignant about the wistful look on her face.

Big brother Alan sported a smile that actually looked painful, as though it might have to be sandblasted from his face. Davenport had photographed him gazing at Laura more often than not, although she appeared oblivious to his attentions.

Brad Goldwyn, by contrast, seemed intent merely on having a good time. Although a little rough around the edges and perhaps uncomfortable in his elegant surroundings, he appeared to have made an effort to fit in, socializing with each of the others in turn. He looked happy and relaxed, in particular in a photo taken with Laura and Tiki, the three standing close together, their heads nearly touching, as though they were sharing a secret.

As for Gary, the best man's mood was mercurial. In one photograph he would be laughing; in the next, scowling. And there was a remarkable series of five consecutive shots in which he and Sean were toasting each other with bottles of champagne. In the first frame, they were smiling as their bottles clinked. By the second, they were drinking. In the third, Sean had looked away, at something or someone off-camera, while Gary took another swig.

In the fourth frame, Sean had taken a step to his right and Gary's expression had darkened, the corners of his mouth turning down. The last shot was of Gary alone, his eyes narrowed, staring grimly in the direction Sean had gone.

"Someone's not a happy camper," Sydney mused, studying the fifth frame.

The sixth negative on the strip was of the bride and groom, with Laura captured in mid-sentence as Sean listened, head down. Of course, there was no way to determine how much time had passed between the fifth and sixth shots, but her impression was that it hadn't been long, since Sean was still holding the champagne bottle.

Had he just walked away from Gary, perhaps after having been summoned by his new wife? *Choosing sides?*

Interesting.

Randy appeared in the final group of negatives, looking young and every inch the heartbreaker he'd turn out to be, but distinctly out of his element in a black leather jacket and jeans, hanging back, more of an observer than a participant.

Except . . . the very last photograph Davenport had taken was of Randy kissing the bride on the cheek while Sean was looking the other way, watching as Alan poured champagne in his glass. But the kiss looked innocent enough, and Laura and Sean were holding hands.

Frozen in time, perhaps just moments away from an awful destiny . . .

Very interesting, indeed. And yet none of the photographs really amounted to a smoking gun. The underlying tension was visible, if you knew what to look for, but the pictures merely brought into sharp focus what she'd already learned.

Although . . . putting it all together, there *were* pieces of the puzzle that fit more snugly than others. The conversation between Laura and Sean, the missing keys, and even those real estate banners flapping in the wind along an otherwise deserted road.

Echoes of the past.

If you don't tell him, I will, Laura had said.

Let me do this my way.

I don't think you want to do it at all.

Put a stop to what, Sydney wondered. She had a strong suspicion, but she needed proof. What was she missing? What had she overlooked? And why did she have the feeling that the answer was staring her in the face?

Feeling restless, she got up and went into the dining room, where she'd worked last night and again this morning, reading and re-reading the old police reports, Laura's journal, Xavier's notes, and her own, and stood there, momentarily overwhelmed by the sheer volume of information.

It was precisely because there was *so much* information,

she thought, that she had missed . . . had missed . . .

The obvious.

Sydney blinked, startled.

It had been after midnight when she'd completed the time-line and she reached for it now. Scanning it quickly, she saw the discrepancy that she had overlooked last night. A little matter of an hour or so, unaccounted for.

Sean and Laura had left the Foster residence for their honeymoon shortly after five o'clock. Xavier had come upon the car on that deserted road at approximately seven P.M., three hours into his shift. He'd told her the radiator was still hissing when he got there.

It wouldn't have been if they'd been broken down on the road for an hour or more, as she had assumed. As the police had assumed. She'd been wrong about that, and that changed everything. That and . . .

"I'll be damned," she said, as the pieces began to click into place.

Twenty-Four

Sydney made several phone calls, laying the groundwork for her plan . . . and baiting the trap.

The first was to Alan Foster. A woman answered his phone—his date from last night?—and when Alan came on the line a minute later, he sounded as if he'd been woken from a deep sleep.

Sunday afternoons had that effect on some people.

"I'm sorry to bother you," she said, "but I think I'm close to finding the person who murdered Sean and Laura, and I need to know—"

"What? Who?"

"I can't say, not until I'm sure. I need to know if you recall where Sean was planning to build the health spa."

There was silence at his end for a minute or more. When he finally answered, his tone was shrewd and a little wary. "It's been a long time," he said, "and you understand I never went out there—Hell, as far as I know Sean only went there once—but the plans I saw were for a four-hundred-acre parcel north of town."

"Can you be more specific than that?"

"Not much. My guess is if you were to drive around in the desert till you found *the* place where you'd least like to spend a week at—some godforsaken spot where you'd be up to your ass in scorpions, rattlesnakes, and coyotes—that's probably it."

"Right."

"But who—"

"Sorry, Alan, I've got to run. Catch you later." She hung up before he could protest and checked his name off her list. The second call was to Smokey's Bar & Grill.

Shouting to be heard over "Chantilly Lace" which was blaring from the jukebox, she asked the bartender a single question: "Is Randy Leighton there?"

The answer did not surprise her.

She tried Tiki next and reached Hortensia, who advised her that Tiki was doing a private reading and could not be disturbed. It took some fast-talking on her part, but Sydney managed to convince Hortensia that it was extremely urgent, and she agreed to take a note in to Tiki. Waiting for the reply, she drummed her fingers on the tile counter, impatient to get on with it.

"Sydney?" Hortensia said, returning to the phone. "Tiki said to tell you that yes, he did. And one more thing—which she said you'd understand—that Laura was driving the Toyota that day."

Sydney thanked her and hung up.

Finally, she dialed Gary West's number. There was no answer.

Sydney parked the car by the front steps and made a point of loading her surveillance equipment and camera bag in the trunk in plain view of anyone who might be watching. She hoped that Tiki was right, and that she was being followed, because it was an essential element of her plan.

She took her time, opening the cases to check the equipment, hoping to impress whoever was watching with the sophistication of her methods, and never mind that she didn't actually anticipate the need for more than one of her high-tech toys.

Besides, it never hurt to be prepared, just in case.

The only tool of her trade that she didn't display was the .38 Special, which she had previously hidden under the driver's seat. Although the killer was almost certainly armed, he would no doubt prefer that the balance of power was tipped in his favor; like a lot of cowards, he wasn't looking for a fair fight.

She didn't want to scare him off.

After a quick stop at 7-Eleven for a six-pack of Calistoga Mountain Spring Water, Sydney set out for the Reno Police Department, keeping an eye on her rearview mirror. It was half-past five, and traffic was virtually at a standstill, with all of the cruisers and car enthusiasts heading out of town.

The party was over, in more ways than one.

Nevertheless, she thought she could pick out her tail, this time driving a later model, dark blue Honda Prelude, its dark-tinted windows shielding the driver from view. The Honda was lurking three cars back, behind an apple green 1932 Austin, from whose windows was blaring "Love Potion No. 9."

She had to give him credit for changing cars; it was human nature to look for trouble from the same source. If he thought she'd seen him last night, he might reasonably expect her to be watching out for a van.

Then again, she might have been mistaken about the van in the first place. Hollywood bad guys were partial to vans, and there was something slightly ominous about the vehicle's hulking size and shape. Vans were, inevitably, the "suspect vehicle."

But not today. She took a right on 2nd Street; the Honda

did likewise. At Center Street, the light turned yellow as she entered the intersection, and a quick glance in the mirror confirmed that he'd caught the red.

He didn't run it.

He had a little self-control, then. Resisting the urge to run a light to keep from losing a target wasn't easy. That suggested that he might have some experience at what he was doing, enough to be confident of his ability to keep her in sight.

For her part, she made no attempt to slow down. She was a little concerned that he might actually lose her, since according to the map she'd memorized, 2nd Street veered off to the right a few blocks further on, and the odds were fifty-fifty he'd continue straight on Kuenzli.

She needn't have worried. As she passed the fire station, she saw that he was behind her again, one car back, with a clear view of the Probe. "Good for you."

Driving past the police department a moment later, she signaled to make a left turn onto High Street. There she parked in front of a bail bonds office, across from the plasma bank. The Honda continued straight on 2nd and made a right turn at the next corner, which would be Park Street, if memory served.

She got out and walked towards the police station. This was the tricky part; she wanted to up the ante, tipping her hand just enough to make him anxious without giving him cause to cut and run. If he thought she was ready to go to the cops with her suspicions, that might convince him that the time had come to act.

Not that she had any intention of talking to the police. Which was why she'd come here; a quick call to Jim Wagner had elicited the information that the main station was closed on Sundays, although the substation on North Center Street was open till seven if she needed to make a report. She hung up before Wagner could ask any questions. He'd only try to stop her—or get in the way.

She hoped he was watching as she passed the chain-link fence around the yard where the patrol cars were parked. She hoped he was watching as she walked up to the station door and tried the door. And she sincerely hoped he was still watching as she pantomimed her frustration at finding it locked.

With a glance at her watch, she headed back to the car.

As she neared Park Street a few minutes later, she saw the Honda laying in wait at the corner. It pulled into traffic after her, taking cover behind a cement truck.

Satisfied that she had piqued his interest, she made a left on Wells and headed for I-80. At the height of the Wells overpass she was momentarily distracted by the curious manifestation of a black Volkswagen Beetle, transformed by the addition of six triple-jointed legs into a wicked-looking spider, squatting malevolently atop a building off to her right.

Another of Reno's many charms, she thought, imagining that it had come up from the desert north of Las Vegas, where the atomic testing had been conducted, after mutating like the giant ants in "Them!"

A minute later, she took a right to the eastbound freeway on-ramp.

The Honda followed.

At the interchange—what locals called the Spaghetti Bowl—she caught 395 north, in the direction of the murder site. On the long, curving access ramps, she lost sight of him, and she held her breath for a few seconds, waiting to see if he would stay with her, if he in fact had guessed where she was going.

The prospect of returning to the scene of his crime after all these years might spook him, and she had to hope his confidence level was such that he'd risk a confrontation in the desert. Although given the isolation of the place, he had to know that it was unlikely anyone would happen by to see him . . . just as she knew there'd be no one coming to her rescue if she was in over her head. For a fleeting moment, Sydney wished she'd asked Wagner for backup. And yet, with anyone riding bodyguard, the killer wouldn't venture near or give himself away.

What she was counting on was that he'd feel he had an insurmountable advantage dealing with her alone. And then, *perhaps* he'd get a little careless.

Her eyes drawn repeatedly to the rearview mirror, she drifted in the lane and had to swerve to keep from clipping the outside guard rail, which looked as though it did yeoman's duty, shepherding inattentive drivers through the curve.

She merged into traffic and shortly thereafter saw the Honda, a few hundred yards back. "Good," she said. "Follow the leader."

As she neared the numbered exit, she noticed that the Honda had disappeared.

"Damn." It might be that he knew where she was going and wanted to put some distance between them so that no one would notice him following her when she left the highway. Worst case scenario, he could be chickening out.

Indeed, as the Probe coasted down the long off-ramp, the road behind her was empty, the pavement shimmering in the late afternoon heat. At the stop sign, she was tempted to wait a few seconds and see if the Honda would show.

She decided against it and made the left turn. Eager as she was to take a peek back at the off-ramp, she kept her eyes straight ahead. Driving slowly as she approached the under-pass—after which the off-ramp would no longer be in view—she turned off the air conditioning and lowered the power windows, the better to listen for the sound of another car.

But there was nothing.

"Damn it," she swore under her breath, tightening her grip on the wheel as she steered around the first of many pot-holes. "Where are you?"

She told herself that he was simply being cautious, that he knew where she was headed and thus felt no need to keep her in sight. Traffic had thinned to a trickle since they'd passed Red Rock Road, and maybe he felt he was too exposed on that near-empty highway.

Chances were, he was parked somewhere along the shoulder, giving her time to maneuver through this obstacle course. It made sense to do so, since otherwise he would catch up with her far too soon and give up the element of sur-prise.

What brought up the goose bumps on her arms, even in the ninety-degree heat, was that if that were the case, it more than likely meant he had driven down this road in the recent past. How else would he possibly know of the road's deterio-rating condition?

Had he made trips to the murder site over the years?

Or had he only come here after the skull was found to as-sure himself that no one had found the place where he'd fired the bullet into Sean's head?

It was a disturbing thought.

Sydney slowed even further as she crossed over the cattle catcher. Getting close, now. Around her, the desert was still, and as desolate as ever. The sun was low in the western horizon, the sky a deep blue, the air clear, the light softer, shadows reaching east from the low brown hills. The scent of sagebrush was so thick in the air she could almost taste it.

The bend in the road was just ahead.

Sydney braked to a stop where she estimated Sean had, fifteen years ago. She turned off the engine, retrieved the .38, and got out. She stuck the gun at the small of her back and pocketed the car keys.

The sound of insects was more noticeable than it had been the other day. This time there wasn't even a hawk in the sky.

Standing in the middle of the road, she shaded her eyes with her hand and turned slowly in a circle, scanning the desert in all directions. There wasn't a sign of the Honda on those few sections of road she could see, but for some strange reason, she was suddenly sure that he was out there . . . waiting.

Watching.

This was a game he had played before, she reminded herself. The last time he'd played, he'd won. What he didn't know was that the rules had changed. He was about to find that out . . . if he came after her.

In her mind, Sydney heard Jim Wagner's stern warning: *You aren't planning to come back here on your own, are you? Because I have to tell you, the desert is no place for a woman alone.*

Technically, though, she wouldn't be alone. Not if *he* was coming after her.

In case he was watching her, even now, from some unknown vantage point, she retrieved her camera from the trunk and began taking pictures.

It was nearly sunset.

Twenty-Five

The shadows lengthened, the sky promised twilight, and still he didn't come.

Her instinct was that he was waiting for the cover of dark. Perhaps he'd grown more cautious as the years passed, and was concerned that this was a setup, in which the police were already involved.

For all she knew, he had set out on foot to walk the perimeter, reassuring himself that they were out here alone and that the cops weren't hiding in the bushes. And at the same time, getting the lay of the land.

Or it could be simply that he hadn't decided, as Tiki had said, whether or not she represented a genuine threat to him. He'd gotten away with murder for all these years, after all, and that fact alone might temper any impulse to strike out.

There was precious little hard evidence in this case, and he probably knew it. As clever as he'd been then, was it any wonder that he would be just as canny now? He could afford to sit tight for awhile; the boy wasn't about to do anything rash.

Unless she pushed him. This wasn't a man who had a lot of use for or respect for women. She was counting on his ego to trip him up.

Regardless, Sydney was uncomfortably aware that he was *out* there, watching. There was always a chance that he'd take a shot at her from cover, in which case, she was a sitting duck. But she figured him to be a hands-on killer. Stabbing Laura, of course, fit that conclusion, but he'd also shown his colors by shooting Sean at close range.

That had to have taken a steely kind of nerve, shooting his best friend in the face. An involuntary shudder ran through her. What if she was wrong? What if he was taking aim right then, ready to pick her off?

"Gary," she called before she lost her nerve. She walked around the car to the trunk. "I think we should talk."

There was only silence; even the bug noise stopped momentarily.

She unlocked the trunk and retrieved the night-vision goggles. They were one of Xavier's favorite toys, less powerful than the bulky version that the military used, but adequate for short distances. They were also sleek and streamlined, and in the dark it would not be obvious that she was wearing them. All else being equal—not that it necessarily was—she could use an edge.

The sun had begun its descent behind the Sierra, and the light would be fading fast. The moon was already out, but for the moment, it was obscured behind clouds that had come out of the east.

"I think I know what happened that day," she said. She slammed the trunk and walked back to the front of the car, boosting herself up to sit on the left front fender, feeling the heat through her jeans. The .38 pressed against her spine and dug unto her flesh, but knowing that he could be watching every move she made, she ignored the discomfort. "I have a theory, Gary, about why you did it. Tell me if I'm wrong."

There hadn't been any wind, earlier, but it picked up suddenly, raising a cloud of dust that swirled skyward and then dissipated.

Was she talking to the wind? She hoped not.

"It probably started as a minor irritation. You were annoyed at Laura for suggesting that Alan be the best man. Sean had already asked you, of course. You were best friends. Had been best friends since the third grade.

"He picked you for kickball, and no one dared laugh or say a word about it. Isn't that what you said? So you were close all through school, even when he was dating Erin. But she was part of your clique; she didn't try to take him away, didn't make him choose."

Her mouth was dry, and she paused, listening. The quiet was unsettling. Menacing.

"Erin was willing to share, for whatever reason. Then she started college, and they drifted apart. It was just the two of you again, and you began making plans.

"You were full of ideas, and Sean had a trust fund. It was a match made in heaven, wasn't it? I don't know where or why the bank came into it, but if they said no, the trust fund was there as a safety net.

"Except at some point, Laura Clifford showed up. Erin says that Laura was a gold-digger, out for Sean's money, but doesn't that also apply to you?"

Sydney paused again to see if he would respond to her taunt. The silence made her wonder if she was out here alone, if she'd miscalculated—

Then she heard a muffled *snap*, like a twig breaking. It sounded as if it had come from down the road, around the bend, although in the fading light she couldn't make out anything clearly. She reached for the goggles, then stopped short. If West was coming closer, she didn't want to give him a reason to change his mind, and there was still enough light for him to see . . .

"But that was business, wasn't it? You were going to be

rich before the year was out, isn't that right? Sean already was, and maybe it didn't matter as much to him, but the spa was a golden opportunity for you.

"That changed, I'm sure, when Sean asked Laura to marry him. All of a sudden, Laura had a say in his future plans. She took a draft of your business proposal to Alan, who told her that spa was a pipe dream.

"That might have been sour grapes on Alan's part, but nevertheless, she objected. She wanted Sean to back out of the deal."

In a few minutes, she estimated, it would be fully dark. This far from the city lights, night fell hard and fast, with only a hint of daylight silhouetting the mountains in shades of pink and orange. Unless the moon peeked from behind the clouds . . .

"I don't know how adamant she was about it, but my guess is that when you showed up at the wedding with Erin, that was the last straw. I have a witness who heard Laura and Sean arguing. She wanted him to 'put an end to it' and he said he would. He was reluctant to do that, to go back on his word, and she accused him of not wanting to do it at all, but . . . it's pretty obvious that he gave in.

"When did he tell you, Gary? When you went outside after the scene with Randy? How did he break the news that Laura wanted him to pull out of your deal? How did he tell you that your dream had died?"

She fell silent again, listening hard over the pounding of her own heart.

The silence was broken by the distinctive sounds of boot heels on pavement, coming her way.

Holding her breath, Sydney reached around to her back for the .38. She put it beside her right leg, trusting that he wouldn't be able to see it there, and waited.

"You don't know shit," Gary West said, coming into sight, slowly walking towards her. He stopped about thirty feet away, a dark shape among many. "And worse than that, you don't know that you don't know shit."

"That's not exactly true." He was holding a gun, she thought. "I know a few things. For example, I know you took Laura's keys."

"What in the hell would I want with her keys?"

"She had a four-wheel-drive Brat; you thought you might need to go off-road, and as it turned out, you did. You had to drive Sean back in the hills and dump the body. You didn't want him to be found right away."

"He was my best friend."

"And he let you down. In the end, he chose her. He told you the deal wasn't going to happen. There'd be no fancy new cars, no nothing."

"Never happened," he said. "You don't know what you're talking about."

"I think I do. You made off with her keys, but I've been told that Sean had a set, and he followed her back to her apartment, so she could park her Toyota there. That's what I missed—what even the police missed—the fact that Laura had driven herself to the wedding that day. Since her car wasn't left at Douglas Foster's house, that could only mean she and Sean did *not* leave directly for the honeymoon after the reception. They were still in town at six o'clock, which in turn means it doesn't matter who was driving what that day; you had plenty of time to switch cars."

"You've lost me."

"Sure I have. Sean drove his Mustang to her apartment. Laura was in the Toyota, and you followed them in your little MG."

"MGB-GT," he corrected.

"Whatever. They went inside, and you loosened the clamp on the radiator hose, drained off some of the water. Hot as it was, you knew they wouldn't get too far before the car overheated. And when they finally left, you followed them in Laura's Subaru."

"Sounds like I was a busy boy."

"You tailed them like you tailed me here today, keeping your distance and waiting for the right moment. But as soon as they got off the highway onto this deserted road, you had them. They were at your mercy . . . except that you had none to offer."

"And exactly how did I arrange it so they took this road?"

"That was pure luck. Good luck for you, bad for them. If Sean had stopped on the highway, I've no doubt you would have driven right by them, and blown it off. Another time, another place. Or maybe you'd have gotten over it. But there were banners along the road, and Sean probably thought he could get help out here."

"In the middle of nowhere?"

"You knew this area better than he did. My guess is the land you wanted to buy for the health spa is nearby."

"Sounds to me like you're doing a whole lot of guessing, and nothing more."

"Sometimes it works that way." She heard a scraping sound, like he had turned on his heel, and, taking a chance that he couldn't see her any better than she could see him, she brought the goggles up quickly and slipped them on. Adjusting the central focusing drive, she saw he was moving, an eerily lit figure in the artificially brightened landscape. "But that should be easy to verify. Maybe Sean thought that's where he was going. He'd only been out here once."

"Don't ask me," West said, taking another step to her right. "I wasn't there."

"I thought at first that he'd left Laura here while he went to try and find some water, probably walking towards the turnout. Five minutes, maybe less, he'd be out of sight, and too far away to run back if he heard Laura cry for help."

"That doesn't make sense. He would have heard a car coming. Sounds carry pretty well out here."

"You're right. They do. One of the things that bothered me all along was why he would leave Laura out here all alone. Even if he thought he could find water nearby, why not take her with him?"

"You tell me," West said.

"Because he didn't leave her. Wouldn't leave her. They were together when you drove up in her car."

"Whoa! Like the cavalry."

"Not exactly. Although I'm sure that's what Sean thought in the beginning. Maybe he wanted to stay behind with the car, while you drove Laura to get help. But Laura knew. She wouldn't get in the car and go with you."

"Well, she could be a bitch," he said, almost philosophically.

"And Sean would never leave her behind . . ."

"The devoted husband."

She couldn't see him smirk, but she heard it in his voice. "Right up to the moment you shot him in the head."

"That must have been a nasty surprise."

"I'm sure it was." West was on the move again, taking careful sideways steps, and she knew he was working up his nerve. "My guess is, *he* was in the car at that point, because they never found any of his blood on the road. All three of you were supposed to go, but . . . she still wouldn't get in the car. She knew, and she was terrified. Laura watched you shoot him, and he was already dead when you went after her with the knife."

"I must be a vicious son of a bitch, shooting my best friend, attacking a defenseless woman for no reason—"

"You had a reason. You hated her from the outset. I imagine the feeling was mutual."

"Like I cared."

"I think you did. It was only a matter of time before she would have convinced Sean that you weren't such a good friend, that he'd be well rid of you. Losing the money was bad enough, but being closed out . . . left out . . . that would be worse."

"If you say so."

"She was the cause of it, nothing but trouble from the day he first saw her."

He laughed again. "Well, that much is true. She wasn't good enough for him, anyone could see that. Teasing and flirting with every man she met . . . and that dance with the kid, like they were fucking standing up."

"For that you killed her? Stabbed her in the heart?" West had stopped, roughly at a forty-five degree angle from her, maybe ten feet away.

West snorted. "We all have to die sometime."

"Ah, that's right. You're not one to mourn the dead."

This time it was West who fell silent.

"When you were done with her, you drove him into the desert, dumped his body and left it for the coyotes. I don't understand that, Gary. How you could leave your best friend to be picked apart. Carrion, left for the buzzards. Did you hate him, too? Because he wouldn't leave her? Because he didn't appreciate what you'd done for him? Or didn't you know that he really loved her?"

A sound escaped him, a sound very much like that of an animal caught in a steel-jawed trap.

Sydney saw his arm come up and she flung herself backwards, rolling off the far side of the car, the .38 in one hand, landing hard on her knees. She heard the shot a split-second later, heard a *thunk* as it hit the car.

Hertz would not be pleased.

Hunched down, she moved along the side of the car, then off at an angle away from the road. Keeping low, she ran for cover—or what passed for it—a mound of dirt and brush not far from where Laura Foster had bled to death.

"Don't make me chase you," West called, his voice calm and seemingly devoid of emotion. "I have nothing against you personally—"

It took an enormous effort not to laugh.

"—but you understand, I can't let you tell your crazy story to the police."

Sydney located him standing at the front of the car. He held his gun in both hands, up near his right ear, in the classic bad guy posture that she'd always thought was one misplaced step away from a high-caliber ear-piercing.

"Not that you could prove any of what you say. No one saw me do anything."

Which was almost certainly true.

"My only mistake was coming after you. I got a little nervous, I admit, at all the questions you were asking, but I was curious, too."

She brought the .38 up, aimed at his gut. She was reasonably proficient with a gun, but she didn't dare try to wing him, not in the dark, because if she missed, the muzzle flash would reveal her position and give him a clean shot at her.

"No, I have no one to blame for this but myself. The funny thing is, time goes by and you forget the details that you'd have sworn were burned into your brain. Petty details, like what you did with the damned key ring."

He was putting one foot in front of the other as though he

were walking the line in a field sobriety test. If his course stayed true, he'd eventually pass within six feet of where she lay in the dirt.

"I think I threw the damned thing away, but I don't remember. I might have kept it as a souvenir, something—" he laughed "—to remember her by."

"Keep talking," Sydney muttered under her breath.

He made slow but steady progress, coming in her direction. "I should have left it with Sean. I mean, he's the one who killed her, really. All he had to do was tell her to butt out. All he had to do was be a man."

Sydney removed the goggles; he was so close now that they were ineffective. She was startled to discover that she could see him now, which meant that he should be able to see her. She glanced up.

The moon was near the edge of the clouds.

If he looked down, he would spot her, but he hadn't yet, his attention seemingly fixed on a thick growth of sagebrush maybe thirty feet beyond where she lay.

"But you talk about luck," West went on, passing within a couple yards of her, "that was the real break, the killer. When they couldn't find Sean, and I heard he was a suspect, make that *the* suspect . . . man, I couldn't believe my luck. I knew I was home free. And every day that went by, I was that much further from being found out."

She rolled carefully onto her side, then over on her back, following his progress with the barrel of the .38. She felt vulnerable this way—it wasn't the simplest thing to get to your feet from this position—but she preferred that to losing sight of West. It would be so easy to squeeze off a shot—

"Until you came along."

She could hear his ragged breathing and even smell him— he was so close.

"Now I have no choice. I've been backed into a corner, and it's me or you. Which means, of course, it's gonna be you. Things'll be messy for awhile, with you disappearing, but I know the perfect place to dump your body. Like they say in real estate, there are only three things that really matter. Location, location, location."

The moon floated free of the clouds, and West was dead in her sights. She cocked the hammer, knowing full well that West would hear its distinctive, menacing click, and tightened her finger on the trigger.

"Gary," she said, "don't move."

He stiffened, turning his head fractionally, as if trying to locate her by sound.

"It's over. Put the gun down."

"I can't do that," he said, reasonably.

"Don't make me shoot you. You'd bleed to death before I could get you back to town."

"And that's a bad thing?" West still held his gun near his right ear, and in the moonlight, she could see his fingers flex around the grip.

"I guess that depends on your point of view."

He laughed again. "I hate to disappoint you, but I'm not going to jail—"

It was instinctive. West turned, as if in slow motion, and lowered his arm, aiming in her direction.

She fired once.

So did he.

Epilogue

Somewhere in the emergency department, a child was crying.

Sydney glanced at the clock on the wall, watching the second hand making its relentless sweep—it was 1:17 A.M. They'd arrived shortly before 10 P.M.; she had indeed managed to drag Gary, who was bleeding profusely, to the car, manhandle him into the passenger seat, buckle him in, and drive them both to the hospital.

The last she'd seen of Gary, he was surrounded by a crowd of medical personnel, one of whom cut through his bloodied shirt to reveal the entrance wound on his left side, midway between his rib cage and the waistband of his jeans. Blood soaked his jeans—which were also being cut off—down to the knees.

His skin tone was ashen, and as far as she could tell, he was unconscious.

A second later, a nurse had ushered her into another room. She was able to strip off her own bloody clothes in exchange for a hospital gown. By then she was feeling dizzy and slightly nauseated, and she'd allowed the nurse to assist her in getting up on the gurney, closed her eyes . . . and felt the room spin.

She was dimly aware of a flurry of activity in the room and felt the stick of a needle in her right arm. The dull ache in her left shoulder which she'd managed to ignore, given the rush of adrenaline, asserted itself as a fiery pain that radiated down to her fingertips. She heard the doctor order Demerol, and whether it was the effect of medication, blood loss, or simply her own exhaustion, she escaped into oblivion.

Now she watched the slow drip of IV fluid and tried to will it to drip faster. The emergency room physician, after examining the rather nasty flesh wound that creased her left shoulder, had pronounced her fit but dehydrated, and told her she would be discharged after the IV infusion.

"You got lucky," the doctor had said, stripping off his latex gloves and standing aside so the nurse could dress the wound. "A couple of inches—the bullet splinters bone, there's vascular and potential nerve damage, and you lose function."

"I feel lucky," she said, wincing at the sting of the antiseptic.

"As it is," the doctor continued as he scribbled on her chart, "you lost some flesh, you'll be sore, a little stiff, and you'll have a scar and a story to tell the grandkids."

"First things first," the nurse had said, winking at her. "There's no hubby listed on her admitting sheet. Let the girl get married before you have her bouncing a grandchild on her knee."

"Ah, but time is fleeting." The doctor put the clipboard on the counter, slipped his pen into the breast pocket of his white lab coat, and smiled at Sydney as he headed for the door. "What are you waiting for?"

Good question, she thought.

"Is there anyone I can call for you, hon?" the nurse asked after he was gone. "A family member? A friend?"

"No one locally, but thanks. A long distance call from the emergency room is probably not the kind a mother would welcome in the middle of the night."

"True enough," the nurse said as she applied a final length of tape along the bottom edge of the sterile dressing. "Anyway, you'll be good to go, as soon as you're re-hydrated. You've got, what? Maybe another 200 milliliters to go."

Sydney opened and closed her right hand repeatedly, in the vain hope that doing so would speed up the process; the IV fluid was cool and her arm felt cold. "I don't suppose you can tell me how Gary West is doing?"

The nurse pulled the silver treatment table away from the bedside. "All I can say is that he's still in surgery. That, and the cops are here to see you."

Frank Micelli, accompanied by a female uniformed deputy carrying a black camera bag, and—bless him—Jim Wagner, came in a few minutes later. Wagner gave her a surreptitious thumbs-up, then came to the head of the bed and assumed a sentry's position, his arms folded stalwartly across his chest.

"I was beginning to wonder when you'd stop by," Sydney said to the sergeant.

Micelli's expression indicated he was not amused in the least. "I've *been* here . . . that battle-ax nurse wouldn't let me in."

"Quality health care in action," Wagner said dryly.

"Or obstruction of justice, depending upon your point of view." Micelli flipped open a dog-eared notebook, clicked his pen, and frowned. "So what's your story, Ms. Bryant? I assume you have one."

"I have one—"

"But," Wagner interrupted, "she probably should wait until her attorney arrives. Just to be safe."

She looked up at Wagner. Now that she thought about it,

it was somewhat surprising that he would be here at all, although she supposed Micelli might have agreed—no doubt reluctantly—to allow his former partner on the case to stand in as a professional courtesy. "I have an attorney?"

"You do. I called Xavier. He called Douglas Foster, who contacted his attorney, who should be arriving any minute now."

"Interesting." Sydney noticed that Micelli's ears were turning a dusky shade of red. "Am I in trouble here?"

"That depends. You shot a man."

"Whoa!" Wagner said. "No Miranda?"

"Technically, she doesn't need Miranda," Micelli said. "This isn't custodial interrogation. It could be self-defense, which isn't a crime. If so, she's not a suspect so there's no need to lawyer-up."

"Technically, you can kiss my—"

"It's okay," Sydney said. "I have nothing to hide."

The door opened behind Micelli, and a Hispanic woman, dressed austerely in a tailored black pin-stripe suit, white blouse, and black and white spectator pumps came into the room. She wore titanium-framed glasses and was carrying a slim attaché and a cell phone. She glanced at each of them in turn, hesitated for only a heartbeat, then said, "I'd like to speak to my client. Alone."

"I don't mind giving the police a statement," Sydney said after she'd outlined the essential elements of her investigation, followed by a brief summary of what had happened in the desert.

"Of course you'll give them a statement," Angela Ochoa said, looking up from her notes. "In due time. You won't earn any Brownie points for doing it sooner, so you might as well get some rest and do it later. And I think it would be a good idea to allow the police to take their own photographs of your injuries."

She had a vague recollection of hearing the distinctive sound of a Polaroid camera not long after she'd arrived at the hospital. "Is that—"

"Necessary? Maybe not, but we'll err on the side of caution. Besides, it takes time for bruises to develop fully, and you've got some colorful abrasions as well. You were fighting for your life . . . photographic evidence will show that."

Sydney closed her eyes. She could still feel the sensation of her finger tightening on the trigger, feel the recoil, see the flash, smell the gunpowder . . . it had happened so quickly and yet had taken forever. "How is he, do you know?"

"Well, he's out of surgery. I believe he's been admitted to Intensive Care. He's in guarded condition, not critical. He hasn't been able to talk to the police, but assuming he will eventually, we want to cover all the bases, make sure he doesn't have any wiggle room."

"It'll be my word against his, I suppose."

"Initially, but we've also got the keys, the Subaru—"

"If anyone can find them." For some reason, Sydney felt compelled to play the devil's advocate. There was, she knew, a huge difference between solving a case and proving it in a court of law.

"As you said, people seldom throw away keys. I've got a drawer full of keys at home, heaven only knows to what. The Subaru . . . my guess is he abandoned it somewhere, maybe stripped it first, removed the license plate and VIN tag, whatever."

"It's not much to go on."

Angela Ochoa smiled. "I've had far less. Don't forget, he came after you with a gun. We should be able to prove that he fired at you twice. And he admitted to you that he killed them."

"Which he'll deny."

"Maybe, maybe not. Regardless, you're a credible witness. So . . . I'll talk to the district attorney, assure him that we'll cooperate fully in the investigation and prosecution, if there is one, but . . . even knowing what to look for, fifteen years later, it'll take some time to check all of this out. I need you to hang tight for a day or two at least."

"I can do that," Sydney agreed, even though she was suddenly anxious to go home to San Diego, anxious to sleep in her own bed.

She settled for a ride back to the condo, arriving as the sun peeked over the brown desert hills to the east. It wasn't home, she thought, letting herself in, but it was blessedly quiet and private, and for now that was enough.

She felt almost numb with exhaustion. Sleep beckoned, but first she took a rather awkward shower, taking care not to get her bandaged left shoulder wet. Her knees were bruised and she had contusions on both shins—no doubt from rolling off the car. She had countless little nicks and cuts on her hands, probably from dragging Gary West through the sagebrush, across rough ground.

Wishing she had pajamas, she slipped instead into a T-shirt, soft cotton shorts, and slouch socks, then climbed in bed. Pulling the covers up to her neck, she began to shiver, although not from being cold.

Sleep eluded her. After a while she got up, found the small plastic bottle of pain pills she'd gotten from the hospital pharmacy, took one, and promptly crawled back into bed. She was still shaking. She closed her eyes, counting the minutes until the medication took hold. It seemed to be taking a long time.

What she really needed was someone's arms around her, a warm body next to hers, what Xavier had called "a human touch."

"What are you waiting for?" the doctor had asked.

It was, Sydney thought, the ultimate sixty-four thousand dollar question. To which she'd never had an answer . . . until now.

She sat up and reached for the phone. When he answered, she said in a rush, "It's Sydney. I know it's early, I know this sounds crazy, but if you want to get married, come on up to Reno . . . now."

He said, "I'm on my way."

MAI